Twin

One month to change their lives!

Identical twin sisters Rowan and Willow may be alike in looks, but both lead very different lives. Dress designer Rowan prefers the anonymity of the Cornish coast, whereas supermodel Willow belongs in the upper echelons of the New York socialite scene. Yet when Willow finds herself needing to hide from the world for a while, she knows there is only one person who can step into her shoes and rescue her—temporarily...

But pulling off their twin swap and trading lives without a hitch is more of a challenge than they anticipated...especially when faced with unexpected romance...!

See what happens when reclusive Rowan steps out of her comfort zone and into the Big Apple and the arms of tycoon Eli while pretending to be her sister in *Cinderella in the Spotlight*.

Available now

And in *Socialite's Nine Month Secret*, after finding out she's pregnant, Willow knows she needs some anonymity for a while to reassess her future— alone. Until she meets the man next door and suddenly her new plan is thrown into delicious chaos!

Coming soon

Dear Reader,

I've always wanted to write a life-swap romance. The idea of leaving your real life and taking on someone else's for a time is just irresistible for me. A chance to do everything you never even dreamed of. To be the person you always thought that maybe you could be, if you just got the chance.

That's not *quite* the way it is for Rowan in this story, though, because the life she's stepping back into is one she already walked away from. But it *does* give her the chance to examine why she ran, and what she ran to—and whether, maybe, she's been hiding from her old life for too long…

I hope you enjoy Rowan's adventures in the Big Apple—and poor Eli's attempts to figure out why the woman he thought he knew from the media and the one in front of him don't seem to match up! But most of all, I hope you find the life that is right for you, wherever it may be—and live that life with your whole heart.

Love and confetti,

Sophie x

Cinderella in the Spotlight

—

Sophie Pembroke

Recycling programs
for this product may
not exist in your area.

ISBN-13: 978-1-335-59658-1

Cinderella in the Spotlight

Copyright © 2024 by Sophie Pembroke

For questions and comments about the quality of this book,
please contact us at CustomerService@Harlequin.com.

Harlequin Enterprises ULC
22 Adelaide St. West, 41st Floor
Toronto, Ontario M5H 4E3, Canada
www.Harlequin.com

Printed in U.S.A.

Sophie Pembroke has been dreaming, reading and writing romance ever since she read her first Harlequin novel as part of her English literature degree at Lancaster University, so getting to write romantic fiction for a living really is a dream come true! Born in Abu Dhabi, Sophie grew up in Wales and now lives in a little Hertfordshire market town with her scientist husband, her incredibly imaginative and creative daughter, and her adventurous, adorable little boy. In Sophie's world, happy *is* forever after, everything stops for tea and there's always time for one more page...

Visit the Author Profile page
at Harlequin.com for more titles.

To anyone who ever wanted to swap their everyday life for something more exciting...

Praise for
Sophie Pembroke

"An emotionally satisfying contemporary romance full of hope and heart, *Second Chance for the Single Mom* is the latest spellbinding tale from Sophie Pembroke's very gifted pen. A poignant and feel-good tale that touches the heart and lifts the spirits."

CHAPTER ONE

ROWAN HARPER LOVED the little fishing village of Rumbelow on the Cornish coast for many reasons—but most of all she loved it because nobody looked at her.

All her life, people had been staring at her. When she was a child, it was because she was standing next to her identical twin Willow, and people couldn't help but try to find a non-existent difference between them. Later, once they hit their teens, it was because they were familiar from billboards and advertising campaigns that seemed to be everywhere, all the time.

Willow said people stared because they were beautiful. Rowan felt that they stared because they were different. Strange. Wrong, even.

Their mother said they should just be grateful that people looked at all, and they'd miss the attention when it was gone—but Rowan knew that was only because *she* missed it, having given up her modelling career to manage theirs instead, when they were just kids.

But here in Rumbelow nobody stared at Rowan, because there were so many other beautiful things to look at. The arc of the harbour as the sun went down. The tiny boats, bobbing on the shimmering waves. The pretty painted houses along the edge of the sea, and the rambling cottages that continued behind it, fanning off the cobblestone streets with their antique shops and coffee houses.

It was the picture-perfect Cornish village, and Rowan had loved it so much the moment she'd set eyes on it that she'd bought the first cottage she'd found and refused to leave.

That had been six years ago.

In those six years, she'd grown accustomed to the rhythms of the place. The spring festivals and summer regattas. The autumn fires and the special pie they had to eat. The Boxing Day swim in the freezing-cold sea. The local folk club playing and singing the same songs they'd played for decades—longer, maybe hundreds of years. Sea shanties and folk tunes that were older than Rowan's thatched roof stone cottage.

This morning, as she swung a straw bag filled with treats from the local bakery over her shoulder and headed back towards the cottage, the only people who noticed her at all were the locals she saw every day, who waved politely.

Despite the community feel of the village, nobody asked too many questions here. If anyone had realised who she was—or who she had been—they never said. In Rumbelow, your life started the moment you arrived in the village, as if nothing that had come before could have ever been important.

Rowan *loved* that.

She took the last turn past the church, out onto the side street that led down the hill to her cottage, right on the outskirts of the village, humming happily to herself. The sun was high in the sky, if not entirely warm this early in the season, and it sparkled on the ripples of the waves as they crested below against the stony beach. This far along, the harbour had given way to a more natural appearance, and Rowan could see right across to the cliffs and the twinkling sails of the boats out at sea.

She smiled to herself, and waved to her nearest neighbour, Gwyn, as he jogged past her towards the town. Gwyn lived all the way around the curve of the harbour in the old converted lifeboat station that was now a luxury seafront property. He frowned and did a double-take before waving back, which confused her.

Until she turned through the gate onto her own garden path…

And stopped.

Because there, on her doorstep, was someone worth staring at.

Someone she hadn't seen in person in six years.

Someone who looked just like her.

'What are you doing here?' Rowan whispered harshly as she fumbled for her keys. The last thing she needed was someone seeing her and her identical twin standing together on the doorstep and putting two and two together.

Not that they looked exactly identical right now. Oh, they both still had the same long blonde hair, wide blue eyes and slender figure—although Rowan admitted the pastries might have caused a small fluctuation there, but she usually offset that with long walks on the cliffs.

But Willow was chicly dressed in wide-legged beige trousers and leather boots, topped with a simple black sweater and a tan leather jacket. Her hair flowed glossily down her back, her manicure was simple but perfect, and even her make-up was flawless.

Rowan was in a turquoise and pink maxi skirt, a white T-shirt and a hoodie, her hair was scraped back into a messy bun, she couldn't remember the last time she'd had a manicure, and all her make-up had dried up and gone in the bin.

No, maybe not so identical right now.

Finally, she managed to get the door open and turned to Willow to usher her inside. 'Come on, come on. Before someone sees you.'

Oh, she hoped that Gwyn hadn't lingered too long on his run down the street. Or that he hadn't noticed the strangely familiar woman standing on Rowan's doorstep for the last...

'How long have you been here?' Rowan asked as she slammed the door behind them.

Willow's eyebrows arched in surprise at the question. 'In England or on your doorstep?'

There was a slight Transatlantic twang to her sister's voice that she'd only heard on the phone before. A consequence of living in New York for so long, Rowan supposed.

'Both.'

Willow placed her large tote bag on the floor beside the telephone table, and Rowan saw her sister frown at the old-fashioned rotary dial phone that sat there. Phone signal was notoriously patchy in the area, so having a landline just made sense—not that anyone really had the number. Which was why she'd figured she might as well have a phone she liked to look at, since it never rang.

'I arrived in England last night,' Willow said, straightening up again. 'I stayed at a hotel near Heathrow, then got a car to bring me down here this morning. I'd been standing on your doorstep for about ten minutes when you arrived. I did try to call, but…'

She gave the rotary dial phone another dubious look.

'Cell signal can be unreliable here.' Rowan carried her own bag down the darkened hall into the brighter kitchen at the back of the cottage, looking out over her higgledy-piggledy garden, then emptied it out onto the kitchen table. 'Croissant?'

Willow looked nauseous at just the idea of carbs, so Rowan grabbed a plate and bit into one herself. No time for jam and butter this morning. She needed comfort food, stat.

'So. Going to tell me why you're here?' Rowan dropped into the wooden chair she'd found at a second-hand shop and painted lavender, to match the plants growing just outside her window. She nodded at the other chair—another thrifted wooden chair in a different style, painted sage-green, and Willow cautiously sat too.

'I need your help,' Willow said.

Rowan reached for another croissant. 'That doesn't sound good.'

Willow had *never* needed her help. Not once.

As kids, Willow had been the ringleader, the one who decided what they were doing and where. And when Rowan couldn't keep up, Willow had made everyone else wait for her. When their mother was worried that Rowan had put on a few pounds and instigated a starvation diet, Willow was the one who sneaked her enough calories to keep going.

When Mum had yelled and screamed at Rowan for not wanting success enough, for being a failure, Willow had calmly stood between them and told her to stop.

When Rowan had started having panic attacks before runway shows, Willow had been the one to practice breathing techniques with her, and run interference so that no one else found out. When Rowan had fainted under the lights on a camera shoot once, Willow had literally caught her when she fell.

And when Rowan had wanted to leave, Willow had supported her. More than that, she'd helped her move her own money away from their mother's control, then booked her the damn aeroplane ticket.

They might not have seen each other in person for six years, but they'd stayed in touch via email and videophone. And Willow was the only person in the world who knew where Rowan had gone when she'd dropped off the radar.

Most importantly, Willow had always, always helped her when she needed it.

Which meant that Rowan knew there was no way she could turn her sister away now.

'What do you need?' Rowan asked, and hoped against hope it wasn't something she wasn't able to give.

Eli rapped his knuckles against the wood of his brother's office door, avoiding the frosted glass pane that read *Ben O'Donnell CEO* in a particularly intimidating font.

Refusing to be intimidated, Eli stuck his head around the door. 'Got a minute?'

Ben was on the phone as usual, so he just

nodded and waved a pen towards the chair opposite his desk. Eli dropped into it and waited.

Since his brother was still making vague noncommittal noises to whoever was on the other end of the phone call, Eli took a moment to study the office. It had a lot of memories, that room. Not so much since Ben became CEO of O'Donnell Industries two years ago—he'd only visited a handful of times, and never for long.

But when their father had ruled the roost…

After their mother left, Eli had spent a lot of time doing his homework at the second assistant's desk outside the room, because at thirteen he was far too old for a nanny, but his father also didn't trust him at home. Ben, at sixteen, had more often been with his friends—or, as far as their father was concerned, involved in school activities. But sometimes he'd come to the company head-quarters building in Manhattan too, and been ushered into the inner sanctum of their father's private office to be initiated in the secrets of how to be a CEO.

At least, that was what Eli had assumed was happening. He was never allowed in to find out.

Growing up, people always told Eli how important his father was, how much his work mattered. People said the same thing about Ben now.

But those same people had also told Eli he was imagining it when he'd worried that his father treated Ben differently to him—loved Ben more than him. His father had said so too, telling him not to be so oversensitive.

He knew now, of course, how right he'd been. As he'd grown up, those same people had stopped trying to keep the whispers from his ears. The ones that said, *'Doesn't he look more like his godfather than his father?'*

They'd still told him he was making it up, though, if he complained about being shut out of his father's office—of his life.

So had Ben, come to that.

Pushing the memories away, Eli got to his feet and strode across the office to the floor-to-ceiling windows that looked out over the Manhattan skyline. No wonder his father had spent more time here than at home, with a view like that.

Not that the view from the family apartment on the Upper East Side was something to be sniffed at either. Even Eli had to admit it had been a wrench to leave that.

'Right. We'll circle back to that on Monday,' Ben said, and Eli guessed his call was coming to an end.

He turned back to head for his designated chair, but couldn't help but look at his brother's desk as he went.

His father had kept it completely clear, excepting only the framed family photo that sat on one corner—a photo that had been removed after Eli's mother left, and replaced with a staged portrait of Ben and Eli instead. Because whatever his father thought in private, in public he would never do anything at all to suggest that Eli wasn't his son.

And if he wasn't…well, both his parents had now taken that secret to their graves, hadn't they?

Anyway, it seemed that Ben had continued his father's clear desk tradition. There, in the corner, the only decoration was a framed photo of Ben and his on-again, off-again girlfriend Willow, at some awards ceremony or another.

Ben was in a tuxedo, and Willow looked impossibly slender and glamorous in a golden gown, her long blonde hair cascading down her back, her famous smile on show. It looked more like a picture in a magazine than a personal shot. Maybe it was, originally.

In his less charitable moments, Eli worried that Ben was more like their father than he was comfortable with.

He wondered too how serious Ben was about Willow—or if he just liked having one of the world's most beautiful women on his arm when the cameras came out. Ben and Willow had been together—sporadically— for a couple of years now, but Eli had never even met her, only seen them together on TV, or in magazines.

He'd seen other women, though, at Ben's flat, or at parties. He'd always assumed that was during the 'off' periods of their relationship, but he'd never asked. He wasn't completely sure he'd like the answer.

Eli pushed the thoughts away. Ben was his brother, after all. He was rich, handsome, charming, and could probably have any woman at the click of his fingers, if he really wanted. If he'd chosen Willow, it had to be for a reason, and Eli had to respect that.

Ben hung up the phone at last and, following the direction of Eli's gaze, turned the photo face down.

Ah. Off-again, then.

'Things not good with Willow at the moment?' He settled back into his chair and slouched down to rest his elbows on the arms, steepling his fingers in front of him. What Ben called his 'therapist pose', although none of the therapists Eli had ever spoken to had used it.

'I got tired of all the demands, you know? Called time on it for now.' Ben leaned back in his own high-backed, top-of-the-range, ergonomic leather desk chair, silhouetted against the Manhattan skyline behind him. He looked relaxed, confident—and still Eli was pretty sure he was lying. Which meant Willow had probably left him, and he didn't want to admit it. It would diminish his reputation, or whatever.

In some ways, he really was just like their father.

Eli had asked his father once why he didn't turn his desk around so he could enjoy the view while he was working. His father had told him that if he was working, he wasn't looking at the view.

He'd asked Ben the same thing when he'd moved in. Ben had simply said it was more intimidating this way.

Eli hadn't been satisfied with either of the

answers. If it had been *his* office, he'd have turned the damn desk around.

But it wasn't. It never would be. Because their father had left executive control of the company, lock, stock and barrel, to Ben. Not that Eli had been left destitute—far from it. Mack O'Donnell would never let it be said he hadn't been generous to his sons—or let anyone suspect he didn't believe Eli to be his biological child. No, Eli might not have got day-to-day control of the company, but he was still technically on the board, even if he never made it to meetings, and he had a share of the family fortune. Eli's father had ensured he'd never have to work a day in his life, if he didn't want to.

But he *did* want to. So he'd made his own way instead.

Which was what had brought him to his brother's office in the first place.

'So if you don't have to escort Willow to any glamorous events this weekend, does that mean you'll have time to look at that file I gave you? The one about the gala sponsorship?'

'Ah, sorry, Eli. I wanted to, really.' Ben flashed him an apologetic smile that didn't come close to reaching his eyes. 'But I promised a certain glamorous redhead that I'd take her out on the boat this weekend instead. *She* only makes one demand of me…and you can probably guess what that is.' He barked a laugh.

Eli forced a smile. If Ben was taking another woman out publicly so soon, that was more evidence he was lying about what was going on with Willow. Overcompensating.

'Perhaps you can take a look before you go,' he suggested. 'Do you have the file here? We could go through it together. Then I really need to take it back with me…' There was sensitive information in that file—information he wouldn't have normally let leave the locked filing cabinet in his office, or the firewall protected data cloud Launch used. But if showing Ben all the details got him interested enough to sponsor the gala event they were setting up that spring—the biggest event his non-profit ran in a year, and bigger this year than ever before—it was worth the risk.

'Uh, I think I left it at Willow's apartment, actually,' Ben said.

Okay. Maybe *not* worth the risk.

'Ben, I told you that file had sensitive information in it.'

'Yeah, yeah, I know. It's not exactly unfamiliar territory to me,' his brother replied. 'I guess it just slipped my mind. You have no idea how much there is to do as CEO of this company.'

No, because Dad never let me find out.

That was an unfair thought. It wasn't Ben's fault that Eli's parentage was doubtful, and their father had cut him out as a result.

'I know how much running a company can take,' he said instead, working hard to make it sound easy and relaxed. He knew Ben didn't consider Eli's own business ventures in the same league as his own—probably because they weren't. 'And to keep mine going, I really need to get that file back.' *And if you're not going to sponsor my event, find someone else who will. Fast.* 'Can you ask Willow for it?'

Ben yanked open his desk drawer and pulled out a key, handing it across the desk to Eli. 'She's out of town, apparently. But you can go grab it yourself. I'll text you the address and the door code. I left it on the counter, I think.'

Eli hesitated before taking the key. He'd never even met Willow, and the most recent information he had about her was that she'd dumped his brother. Invading her apartment in her absence felt wrong, even if it was to retrieve an important file.

'You're sure she won't mind?'

Ben shrugged. 'I'll shoot her a text and warn her you'll be going, if you like.'

Eli reached for the key. 'That would be great. Have fun on the boat this weekend.'

He turned and left the office, feeling the weight lift from his shoulders the way it always did when he escaped that room.

He had work to do.

Rowan made tea as Willow talked, because it helped to have something to do with her hands. When she'd lived in America, it had been all coffee, all the time—black and strong and sometimes the only thing she'd consume all day.

Back in Britain, she'd retrained her tastebuds to love the calming, soothing taste of tea.

Even tea wasn't up to this challenge, though.

'You're *pregnant*?' Rowan plonked one of the mugs of tea down in front of her twin. 'How did that happen?'

It was a mark of how serious the situation was that Willow didn't even make a joke about the birds and the bees, or how long it must have been for Rowan if she didn't remember. Rowan almost wished she would. It would make this less…weird.

'It certainly wasn't planned, I can tell you that.' Willow sighed and reached for her mug, blowing slightly over the surface so steam snaked up towards the ceiling.

'Who's the father? Does he know?' That was the next proper question to ask, wasn't it?

'Ben, of course.' Willow frowned at her across the kitchen table. 'What did you think?'

'Sorry. I just…' She'd never met Ben, of course, but she'd seen plenty of photos of the two of them online or in magazines, appearing at glamorous events or holidaying in exotic places. And Willow had mentioned him often when they'd spoken on the phone, or in her emails and texts. 'I guess I figured that if the father was your long-term boyfriend you'd be talking to him instead of me.'

That made Willow wince and look away towards the window.

Hmm. Definitely something her sister hadn't been telling her in those phone calls, then.

'Things with Ben and me…it's not what I'd call a stable relationship environment. Or anything a kid should be involved in.' Willow's words were flat, unemotional. But Rowan read a world of meaning behind them.

'Does he hurt you? Physically or emotionally? Because you do *not* have to go back to him—'

'It's not like that.' Willow sighed. 'He's… I mean, we're…'

'You're really convincing me here, Will.'

Willow huffed a laugh and looked down at her tea again. 'I know. I'm sorry. It's just…the world thinks we're some fairy tale romance, right? The supermodel and the CEO, living our perfect glamorous life together, madly in love.'

'And it's not really like that?' Rowan asked softly. She'd never seen her sister look vulnerable this way before. Usually, *she* was the one who was falling apart, and Willow was the one holding her up.

Maybe it was about time they tried things the other way around for a change. She certainly owed her.

'You know, some days I'm not sure we even *like* each other,' Willow admitted. 'Right from the start…we were together because it was good for our images, our careers. We look great next to each other, and the papers like to talk about us a lot, and that was kind of what we both needed. We could fake the rest.'

'You *faked* being in love with your boyfriend?' Okay, that definitely sounded like the sort of thing that only happened in the bad romcom movies that Rowan usually watched when she couldn't sleep on stormy nights.

'Not…intentionally.' Willow sighed again. Was all this heavy breathing good for the baby? Rowan didn't know.

Maybe she'd have to learn.

'Okay, tell me the whole story.'

The whole story took another pot of tea and several croissants, but basically boiled down to this.

Willow and Ben had met at some society party and realised that they were just the sort of person the other had been looking for. In Willow's case, Ben was successful in his own right so not intimidated by her success, he was rich enough that she knew he wasn't after her money, and they had a lot of the same friends so would inevitably end up at the same events.

In Ben's case, Willow was recognised by the world at large as being beautiful, and that seemed to be enough for him.

They went out on a date and got photographed by the paparazzi. So they went out on another one, and people started talking about them.

'And now it's two years later, and we've

never really had a conversation about our future, or our feelings, or if we even like each other beyond spending time in the public eye together and having someone there to have sex with whenever we want to scratch that itch.'

'Do you want to?' Rowan asked. 'I mean, do you want to tell him about the baby? See if the two of you can be a real family together?'

It was something neither of the sisters had ever known. Their father had been out of the picture almost before they were born, and their mother hadn't exactly been mum of the year. She'd always been more interested in how much money they could make her than who they were inside.

Maybe that was how Willow had fallen into such a transactional relationship with Ben.

'I...' Willow looked up and met Rowan's gaze, swallowing hard. 'It sounds awful, but I don't think I do. This is the man I spent the last two years of my life with, sort of. But I know—like, deep down, heart knowledge—that he'd be the wrong partner for me in this. That we wouldn't be happy—and neither would our child.'

Well. That was stark enough.

'You still need to tell him, though,' Rowan pointed out. 'Especially if... Wait. I skipped ahead a step. Do you know what you want to do? Do you want to keep the baby?'

Because if she didn't, why had Willow flown across a whole ocean to tell her about it?

Willow nodded. 'I do. It might be crazy, because what about my career and my figure and my life, and I don't have any support in New York, but I guess I can hire that? I don't know. All I know is that I want to be a mom—a better one than ours was. I want to raise this baby right. And yes, I *know* I have to tell Ben. I just… I need to figure some things out first, about how this is all going to work.'

'I can get that.' Finally, something about Willow's arrival here was making sense. She needed a place to hide, to think, to feel safe.

Rowan knew better than anyone how good Rumbelow was for that.

'I just know if I talk to Ben before I've made some decisions about everything…he'll take over. He'll want things all his own way and I won't be sure enough of anything to fight him on it.'

And in that one sentence, Willow had told her more about her relationship with Ben than in the rambling story that took two pots of tea.

Rowan reached across the table and grabbed her twin's hand. 'You can stay here as long as you like,' she told her fiercely. 'We'll figure this all out so you can go back with a plan and do this the way you need to.'

Ben would want to have input, of course, but Rowan wasn't going to let him steamroller over Willow's wishes either.

Willow's face relaxed into a small smile. 'Thank you. I hoped… That will really help.'

'Of course. You're my sister. I'll always be here for you.' Especially given how many times Willow had been there for her.

Rowan got to her feet to put the kettle on one last time, and grab her planner so they could start thinking through the essentials— like doctors' check-ups and whether she actually owned any sheets for the spare room.

But Willow stopped her with a gentle hand on her arm. 'Actually, there was one more thing I needed. It's a lot to ask, but…'

'Anything.'

'I need you to go to New York and pretend to be me. So Ben doesn't get suspicious. I need you to be Willow Harper, supermodel, for a few weeks.'

CHAPTER TWO

WILLOW'S MANHATTAN APARTMENT was pretty much as Eli would have expected it to be—if he'd spent any time at all picturing the home of his brother's sometimes girlfriend, which he hadn't.

Too trendy for a doorman, it had instead some sort of state-of-the-art ID technology that Eli easily bypassed with the code his brother had texted him after he'd left the office the day before. He took the elevator up to the penthouse, barely pausing to take in the stark white and metal industrial chic foyer, or the modern artwork in the elevator itself.

On the top floor there was just one door off the short hallway; Willow clearly had the entire penthouse floor to herself. Eli knocked and waited, just in case. But when there was no response he used the key Ben had given him to let himself in.

Ben had promised to tell Willow he'd be

coming by. Besides, Willow was out of the country at the moment.

There was literally no reason for Eli to feel like he was invading a stranger's privacy.

He did, anyway.

But the apartment was empty, as promised. Eli stood by the door, hands on hips, as he scanned the open-plan space. Huge windows meant most of the walls were nothing but glass from the floor to the ceiling; Eli assumed there must be blinds of some sort, or invisible tinting or something, because otherwise living here had to feel like being watched, all the time.

Standing in Willow's own personal space didn't give him any more of a feel for who the woman was. He realised now that his discomfort at invading her private home was unnecessary; there was nothing private or personal here—at least, not in the main living area. It was all white walls, monochrome art, metal bars and neutral furnishings. Not even a magazine on the wood and metal coffee table to give a hint at the owner's personality.

Maybe the private rooms—bedrooms, bathrooms—were different. But the living space that spanned over half the top floor of the building looked more like an event space than a home—with a showcase kitchen and bar, small sitting areas by the windows, as well as the larger living area, and a glass dining table that could seat almost as many kids as they got down at the Castaway Café on a cold Friday night.

Eli shook his head and got down to business.

Ben had said he'd left the file on the counter. Assuming that Willow hadn't moved it since then, that narrowed things down a bit. There was the kitchen counter, the bar over by the window and a few other shelves with some minimalist decor—and it wasn't as if there was a lot of clutter for it to get lost in. If only he'd put the paperwork in a file that was any colour other than white he'd probably have spotted it already.

Of course, if she *had* moved it...

Eli's stomach clenched as it occurred to him that this was *not* a woman who liked clutter, clearly. What were the chances she'd leave her *ex-boyfriend's* clutter lying around the place after he forgot it? Slim, he reckoned.

If he was lucky, she'd have stashed it in a box with any other of Ben's things. If he was unlucky, it had gone in the trash.

With a sigh, Eli moved into the apartment

and began systematically checking counter spaces then, when that turned up nothing, looking in cupboards for some sort of container of his brother's belongings.

He had his head in a cupboard full of cleaning supplies—all eco-friendly, expensive and in frosted white bottles—when he heard a key in the front door.

Ducking out of the cupboard, he tried to straighten up and brush himself down—but by the time he emerged above the kitchen counter Willow was already staring at him from the doorway, her eyes wide and terrified.

'Sorry! Sorry, Ben said you were away and—'

He was cut off by Willow's scream, and the crash of her bags dropping to the hardwood floor.

Eli dashed around towards her, narrowly missing the glass coffee table, and slid to a stop just in front of her. They'd never met, but surely she'd recognise him from Ben's photos or something?

'Willow! Don't worry, it's just me. Eli. Ben's brother?' He kept his voice as calm and as reassuring as he could, but it didn't seem to make any difference. The panic had got hold of her, and the fear in her eyes wasn't receding one bit.

Now he was closer, he could see that her hands were trembling—no wonder she'd dropped her bags. Her chest was moving rapidly in and out too, her breaths shallow and desperate.

A panic attack. She's having a panic attack—because of me.

Damn Ben and his inability to read a damn file in good time.

Except he couldn't even blame his brother. Because he'd known it was a bad idea to come here and he'd done it anyway, because he needed that file.

He'd caused this. Now he had to try and fix it.

'Okay, Willow?' He moved close enough to meet her gaze, but not so close as to spook her. 'I think you're having a panic attack, or maybe an anxiety attack. Okay? Have you had these before?'

Her pupils darted around the apartment, looking everywhere except at him, but she nodded, just a little.

'I'm going to stay here with you until you're calm again, okay?' Eli went on, still speaking calmly and softly. 'Then I'll leave, once

I know you're okay. But for now, how about I take your hand?'

He held out his hand, palm up, and waited to see if she'd accept it. He knew that, for some people, touch could be grounding. But Willow didn't know him, and for all he knew it could be the opposite of what she needed.

After a moment, Willow reached out and grabbed his fingers, her hand clammy and still shaking.

'Okay. Okay, that's good.' He smiled gently at her. Some people needed quiet to process an attack like this, but for others a soothing voice helped too—and Willow seemed to be responding well to his. 'Shall we sit down?' Another nod.

He turned, about to lead her to the sofa, but she was already sliding down the wall behind her to sit on the floor, so he did the same.

From down there, the apartment seemed even more vast and empty. Eli wasn't surprised she'd had a panic attack finding him there. He was more surprised she didn't have one every time she came home to this place.

The sparse apartment seemed to echo with their breathing as they sat in silence, Willow still gripping his hand tightly. The ends of her loose blonde hair tickled the side of his arm, where he'd rolled his sleeves up. The sensation reminded him of another trick he'd learned to help people suffering from anxiety or panic.

He shifted slightly to face her. 'Are you ready to try something else?'

There was a trust now in her gaze that he hadn't anticipated.

He hadn't expected how good it would make him feel to see that look on a virtual stranger's face either.

Willow nodded, and Eli pushed the thought aside. He was here to help. Not bond with his brother's ex.

The world was starting to come back into focus for Rowan as she sat on the floor of her sister's apartment with…some guy?

A big, broad, gorgeous guy in a suit who was holding her hand.

He'd told her his name, hadn't he? But her heart had been pounding so loudly in her chest, her blood roaring in her ears, that she hadn't heard, or at least hadn't taken it in.

Now she was sitting here clutching his fingers tight, so she should probably make sure to figure out his name at some point.

Also, what he was doing in Willow's apartment when she was out of the country. That seemed like relevant information.

But first, she needed to get her body back on an even keel. God, it had been so long since she'd had an attack as bad as this that she'd almost forgotten what it felt like.

Well, no. That was a lie. She hadn't forgotten. But she'd *wanted* to.

It was just…it had been kind of a day. Or a couple of days.

Ever since Willow had arrived on her doorstep and she'd felt the world shift, it seemed as if she'd been on the edge of something like this. And once she'd realised what her twin wanted her to do…

'Go to New York and pretend to be you?' she'd asked incredulously. *'How could I even do that?'*

'We're identical, Rowan. It'll be easy.'

Willow had sounded so sure, so convinced that her plan would work, it had been hard to argue with her.

That wasn't why Rowan had agreed to it, of course. She'd done that because her sister needed her help for once, and it was well past Rowan's turn to provide it.

Still. What Willow didn't seem to realise was that the identical thing was only skin-deep. Yes, she could still pass for her twin in a photo. But in person? Rowan wasn't so sure.

Even the journey here had made that much clear. Not to mention the packing session beforehand.

She'd pulled out her old battered suitcase from the top of the wardrobe, only to find Willow shaking her head.

'That won't do. You'll have to take mine. No one would ever believe I'd travel with that thing.'

The same proved true about the clothes Rowan had planned to pack, and the skincare products and, well, everything else. In the end, Rowan had been dispatched to Heathrow Airport dressed in her twin's clothes and sunglasses, her suitcase half empty, as Willow told her she could just use her wardrobe and such when she arrived in New York.

New York.

She'd forgotten how busy airports were. How in a hurry everyone was. The way announcements blared out and how a low-level buzz of noise remained constant.

Rowan had been glad of her noise-reducing earplugs at the airport, as well as on the flight. But even they hadn't been enough to protect her against the noise, bustle and chaos of New York in the spring.

Last time she'd been there had been for New York Fashion Week, right before she'd quit modelling, and America, for good. At least Fashion Week was over there for another season, attention moving to other shows around the globe.

Willow had assured her she had no shows booked, no photo shoots even. Mostly what Rowan had to do was leave the apartment often enough to be papped around the city, so people believed she was still there. And by people, Willow mostly meant Ben.

There was a chance she'd get invited out to some events, but Willow seemed confident Rowan could handle those.

Since she was currently battling a panic attack on the floor of Willow's apartment, Rowan was less sure.

Her heart slowed a little at last, her breath rasping less harshly in her chest. The panic was passing, and the fear was setting in to take its place.

Beside her, her companion twisted around to look at her. His eyes were very, very green, she noticed absently. Green eyes under dark hair. 'Are you ready to try something else?'

Aren't I already trying enough new things here?

The thought bubbled up and almost made her giggle, which she was sure would convince him she was having some sort of breakdown, so she held it in. Instead, she caught his gaze and, when she saw only concern and comfort there, she nodded.

Maybe she wasn't sure who this guy was yet, but she was almost certain she could trust him. Willow obviously did, if she'd given him a key to her apartment—a thought her anxious brain hadn't been able to process until now. The lock hadn't been broken, after all, and security on the building was pretty good.

She nodded.

'Okay, let's do some breathing together, yeah?' He waited for her second nod before starting.

Using his free hand, the one she wasn't still clutching damply—and oh, yes, she was going to feel embarrassed about that later—he swooped a finger up towards his face as he breathed in, held it there for a few beats, then flew it away again as he breathed out. It should have looked ridiculous, but somehow his sincerity made it anything but.

Rowan tried to mirror his breathing patterns. Breathing techniques always helped her. It was just hard to remember them when she was in the middle of an attack.

Finally, the weight in her chest lifted and an incredible tiredness swamped her instead. She gave his hand one last squeeze then let it go, trying not to miss the connection the moment it was gone.

'Sorry for, well, that. I hope you didn't need the bones in that hand for anything.' Ah, yes, here came the embarrassment. She could feel the heat rising in her cheeks as she realised what this stranger had just witnessed.

But he shook his head firmly. 'Don't apologise, Willow, please. I'm the one who should be sorry, for surprising you here.'

Okay, so she shouldn't have been expecting him. That was a start. Even if hearing him address her by her twin's name was weirder than she'd expected. It used to happen all the time but, after six years away, she'd forgotten how it felt.

Still, at least that meant Willow was right, and they did still look identical enough to pass as each other. As long as Rowan was wearing Willow's clothes and did her hair properly, anyway.

First hurdle jumped.

Now she just needed to try and figure out who he was without giving away that she wasn't who he thought she was. If that made sense anywhere outside her head.

She didn't know what his connection to Willow was yet, for a start. Was there more to the story than her twin had told her, sitting at her kitchen table in Rumbelow?

'Yeah... I know you told me what you were doing here, but...'

'Of course.' He seemed incredibly understanding, anyway. Rowan suspected he must have had experience with anxiety attacks in the past—maybe supporting a friend through them or something, because he hadn't been fazed at all by hers. 'Ben gave me his key because he'd left a sensitive file here...'

'And he sent you to get it?' So did that make this guy Ben's assistant or something? Because, in that case, they were back to it being very weird that he was in Willow's apartment at all.

But at least he's not potentially the secret father of my niece or nephew.

Not that that idea should have bothered her,

beyond the fact that it would have meant Willow had been lying to her.

'Sort of.' He pulled a face. 'It was my file—it's all the details for this gala event my non-profit organisation is running this spring—you know, Launch? I don't know how much Ben has told you about it, or what you've seen in the press, but we do work among troubled teens in the city—helping with mental health issues, providing refuges and food banks and the like, especially for teen boys who can't go with their moms and sisters to domestic violence refuges.'

'That sounds...great.' She probably didn't sound very convincing, but she genuinely believed it was. She just couldn't figure out what it had to do with Ben or Willow.

'Yeah, but it needs a lot of support every year. And this year we're gunning for something bigger and better than ever, so...' He shrugged, a self-deprecating smile on his face. 'I figured it was time to lean on those old family connections, you know? But Ben left the file here, and now he's away this weekend...' He trailed off, as if afraid he'd said too much.

As if she cared about Ben's plans. Away for the weekend suited her perfectly.

Wait.

Family connections?

This guy was Ben's *family*?

Oh, she needed to get him out of here *fast*.

No matter how gorgeous he was.

Eli wasn't sure exactly what he'd said—maybe she wasn't into charity work? Except who honestly didn't care about other people? Hopefully not someone Ben would have dated for this long—but suddenly Willow was on her feet and eager to get him out of the door.

She wobbled a little when she stood, though.

Eli clocked the suitcases by the door, and the shadows under her eyes—not enough to make her any less beautiful by the world's general standards, but enough to make her look tired.

Tired. She'd just flown in from somewhere, found a man in her apartment and had a massive panic attack.

She had to be exhausted.

'Thank you for sitting with me,' she said with a polite smile. 'But I'm really all right now.' She looked pointedly towards the door.

She sounded more English than he'd expected, considering how long she'd lived in the States now. But maybe the accent was part of her persona.

'Right. I should…get going.' Except he still hadn't found that damn file. 'Um…'

Willow looked blankly at him for a moment, before her eyes widened. 'Your file. Right?'

'Yeah.' He gave her an apologetic smile. 'I'm sorry. I wouldn't bother—I wouldn't have come here at all—except it's really important. And, well, it has some sensitive data in it.'

'Why on earth would Ben leave it here, then?' she asked, looking baffled.

He shrugged. 'You know Ben.'

'Yes. Right. I absolutely do.' She moved into the apartment a little way, towards the kitchen, then stopped and looked around her, as if lost in her own home. 'I don't suppose he told you where he left it?'

'He said he left it on a counter.' Eli stepped closer, behind her, but making sure to keep enough distance to respect her personal space. 'But I couldn't see it anywhere. I thought maybe you might have tidied it away somewhere.'

Willow gave a weary sigh. 'Probably. Come on then, we'd better get looking.'

For an immaculately tidy apartment, it had a surprising amount of storage shelves and cupboards, all of them stocked with clear acrylic containers and organised in rainbow order. Since Willow seemed surprised by their contents every time she opened a cupboard, Eli suspected the place had been sorted by professional organisers—possibly even while she was away.

Finally, they found the file in a stack of creamy folders stood up in an acrylic holder. It took longer than it might have done, as the scribbled on and reused folder he'd grabbed from the office to put the information in for Ben had been replaced by a sleek, shiny nude-coloured one.

Eli flicked through the papers to make sure they were all there and felt his shoulders relax at knowing he had it back. Of course, the fact that professional organisers were potentially the only people to have handled it since he gave it to Ben didn't bode well for his chances of getting the sponsorship he'd hoped for from the family company, but that just meant he'd have to try some other routes. He had contacts. He'd make it happen.

There were kids relying on him.

'Right, well, that's great, then!' Willow swept towards the door, obviously expecting him to follow. 'You've got your file, I'm no longer in a heap on the floor, everything is great! Lovely to see you.'

She opened the front door and held it expectantly.

Eli hesitated. Of course she wanted him to leave, that was totally reasonable. She'd just travelled back from overseas, found him in her apartment and had a panic attack. She'd wanted him to go *before* they had to hunt for the file, and he hadn't expected that desire to have diminished any. Add into all that the fact that she'd just broken up with his brother—again—and her attitude made perfect sense.

Except...he couldn't shake the feeling that there was something more to it. That she wanted him to leave before something else happened.

And, because he was the curious sort, he couldn't help but wonder what that might be.

Willow vibrated with an energy he recognised—a wary, nervous, almost frightened energy. One he saw all the time in the kids who came through the doors at the Castaway Café when he was serving there on one of his volunteer nights.

Maybe it was just the after-effects of the attack. Or maybe it was something more.

Either way, Eli knew he wouldn't feel right

about what had happened here today unless he came back and checked up on her again, soon.

And if the memory of her hand in his, or the way she'd made self-deprecating jokes about the perfect order of her apartment as they'd searched for his file together, made him think that coming back wouldn't be such a bad thing... Well, he was going to ignore those thoughts for now. Because she was his brother's ex-girlfriend, and before long she'd probably be his girlfriend again, and he just wasn't going to go there, even mentally, even for a moment.

'Thanks again for your help.' He flashed her a smile as he held up the file. 'And, you know, for not calling the police on me.'

'You're welcome.' She opened the door a little further.

'I'll get out of your hair now. Goodbye, Willow.'

'Bye...uh...yeah. Goodbye.'

The door slammed so fast behind him that he was almost blown towards the elevator. Eli smiled to himself as he pressed the down button—until something occurred to him, and his smile faded.

He was almost certain Willow couldn't remember his name.

CHAPTER THREE

ROWAN SLAMMED THE door behind her visitor, turned and slid down it to sit on the floor for the second time that day. This time, though, she wasn't having an anxiety attack. She was thinking. Hard.

Groping for her carry-on bag, she fished out her phone—now housed in Willow's sleek taupe case instead of her own turquoise sticker-covered one—and tapped at the screen until it started to ring.

Willow's face appeared almost immediately.

'Are you there? You should have been there *ages* ago. What happened?' It was moderately gratifying to see the concern in her twin's expression. But it didn't eclipse the pang of homesickness Rowan felt when she spotted her familiar, slightly battered kitchen cabinets behind her.

'I'm here,' she reassured Willow. 'The flight and everything was fine—nobody blinked twice at me using your passport either.' Technically, Rowan was pretty certain that was wildly illegal, but Willow had insisted.

'Ben might check flight records or something,' she'd insisted.

Rowan had almost questioned why and how he'd do that, but Willow had been so tense by that point she'd just let it go.

'So why didn't you call before?'

Rowan tipped her head back against the door and closed her eyes. 'Because there was a man waiting in your apartment when I arrived.'

'What?' Willow's screamed word echoed off the almost empty walls of the apartment. 'Was it Ben? What did he say? What *happened*? Rowan, *look at me!*'

With a sigh, she opened her eyes again to look at the screen. 'I'm hoping you can tell me.' She explained everything that had happened, glossing over the anxiety attack as best she could. There was no point worrying Willow when she was all the way across an ocean and couldn't do anything about it.

She also didn't go into too much detail about how gorgeous he was—with his broad shoulders and warm smile and bright green eyes that just begged her to trust him.

She didn't want Willow getting ideas.

'He said he was family? You're sure?' Willow looked thoughtful.

'Very sure,' Rowan confirmed. 'That was when I *really* started to panic. Not— It was fine,' she amended quickly, when Willow's eyes widened with unasked questions. 'I just figured that if anyone was going to know that I wasn't you, a relative of Ben's was probably pretty likely.'

'You'd be surprised,' Willow said drily. 'From the description—and the fact that Ben doesn't actually have a lot of family he's in touch with—I think it must have been his brother, Eli. He runs some sort of charity in the city, I think? I don't really know.'

'Launch,' Rowan confirmed. 'That was why he was here—looking for a file for some event or another. But Will…he was looking at me a lot. Like, suspiciously. I think he might have guessed I wasn't you.'

Willow laughed. 'I doubt it! I've never even met the man in person over the last two years. If I'd walked in on him I might not have recognised him and just called the cops on him. He was lucky he got you instead.'

Rowan thought about how he'd sat beside her and helped her ride out her anxiety attack. How patient and calm he'd been. How he'd known all the right things to say and do. 'Right. Lucky.' She couldn't tell Willow, but *she'd* been the lucky one.

'Seriously, Ro, don't worry. He won't have suspected a thing.' Willow looked a lot more cheerful on the screen now. 'Ben always says Eli's too wrapped up in that non-profit of his to pay any attention to the real world, anyway.'

'Huh.' Rowan was starting to suspect that Willow wasn't the only one who didn't know Eli very well. She'd only spent a brief time with him, under not the best circumstances, but she could already have told Ben that Eli understood the real world perfectly well—at least, the world she lived in.

'Anyway. I wouldn't worry about it. So, how do you like my flat?' Willow smiled proudly across the phone screen. 'Isn't the view fantastic?'

'I, uh, haven't really had a chance to appreciate it yet. Eli just left.' Also, she had a crippling fear of heights, so looking out of those huge windows was not high on her list of things to do for fun.

Willow frowned. 'Where are you, anyway? Are you…is that the front door behind you? Why aren't you sitting on the sofa?'

'Just tired.' Rowan gave a wan smile. 'Just sat where I fell after getting rid of Eli.' Probably better not to mention that she was too scared of marking any of the pristine white furniture to use it yet. She still had to replicate the perfect organisation system Willow had implemented throughout the flat.

Eli had assumed she must have got a professional organiser in, and Rowan hadn't corrected him, since it gave her a neat excuse for why she didn't know where anything was. But she knew her sister. Those clear acrylic containers and that rainbow organisational system was definitely all Willow.

'Well, feel free to make yourself at home there, Ro.' Willow's expression turned serious. 'I know how big a favour you're doing me, and I don't take it for granted.'

'It'll be fine,' Rowan said, hoping it wasn't a lie. 'At least there aren't any photo shoots or shows to cope with.'

She wasn't going to think about the last time she did a modelling shoot. About how she'd fainted under the lights, and the booking agent had said she looked unhealthy and unwell, and her mother had screamed at her backstage so loudly that everyone on the shoot must have heard.

That was the day she'd known she needed to leave.

She'd been contracted for three more runway shows before her twenty-first birthday—the day the money she'd been earning since she was young came into her own hands. She'd gritted her teeth and, with Willow's help, made it through them.

And she'd never gone back. Never spoken to their mother again. Moved countries and changed her whole life.

Now she had to try and remember that old life all over again.

'I mean it, Rowan,' Willow insisted. 'My home is your home. My things are your things. You've got my credit card in your bag—use it. Go shopping. Go out for meals. See the sights. Have an adventure for once. Seriously. If you haven't racked up a massive bill on that thing one way or another by the time we swap back, I'll be seriously disappointed. You know I'm good for the money.'

That was true. Rowan had left America with a healthy bank balance for anyone, let alone a twenty-one-year-old single woman. A large chunk had gone on buying her cottage outright, some she'd invested for the future, and the rest she'd needed to make last.

Her childhood had been spent on modelling shoots, not in a classroom. Their mother had pulled them out of school as soon as they were legally old enough, and it wasn't as if she had much in the way of work experience that wasn't basically looking pretty in different poses.

Except, she'd realised, she did. She knew clothes. She knew fashion. She knew how fabrics draped, and how cuts looked on different bodies. And while she might not want to be the one showing them off any more, she *did* love clothes—the way they could express someone's personality in a glance, far better than any multiple-choice test. How they could provide confidence or take it away. How the cheapest fast fashion could look expensive worn in the right way, and the most high-end designer item could look cheap if worn wrong.

Even when she'd been working, she'd been far more interested in what other people were wearing than the clothes she was being dressed in. She liked seeing how the industry insiders chose their outfits. How stylists and stores interpreted the high fashion trends from the catwalk into something celebrities could wear on the red carpet, and then into something anyone could wear day to day.

She'd paid attention to how the outfits were constructed too—the fittings and the alterations made when she needed a couture dress for an event. The design process fascinated her, and she'd started picking up books on it whenever they had downtime.

So, alone in her little seaside cottage, she'd put all that knowledge to good use. She'd started a style blog at first, anonymously, of course. She'd post photos of her outfits, but laid out on her bed, or if she was wearing them, with her head cut off.

And she'd started making her own clothes too. Things she'd never have worn in New York. She didn't worry about fashion or trends, she just made the things she liked. Like retro headscarves in bright floral fabric. Floaty summer dresses and maxi skirts. Things that made her feel like herself, at last.

She'd fallen into making clothes for other people almost by accident. She'd overheard a teenage girl in tears outside the only formalwear shop in the nearest town, her mother helplessly trying to comfort her. She'd needed a dress for the school prom, and none of them fitted her because she wasn't whatever the shop had deemed to be the perfect size for a sixteen-year-old girl.

Rowan had tried to keep a bit of distance with the local community, but this was different.

She'd offered to make her a dress—and the girl and her mum had been thrilled with it. Mum had insisted on paying, and she'd spread the word too. Soon Rowan had business cards and a simple website and an income again.

She was lucky she'd finished her last commission just before Willow came knocking, or she'd never have been able to disappear to New York for weeks on end.

But now she was here, and with her sister's credit card… She knew exactly what she wanted to do with it.

Eli had been told, often in his life, that he had some sort of guilt complex. First by his brother, then by various ex-girlfriends, and even by a therapist or two—although they generally used much more complex terms.

The meaning was the same. Eli felt guilty. About a lot of things. A lot of the time.

Maybe it was because he'd been born into such privilege when so many others had so little. Or perhaps it was because he knew the circumstances of his birth were suspect, but his father could never admit it. Or maybe it was just how he was.

Whatever the reason, it meant he spent a lot of his time, energy and personal fortune trying to assuage that guilt. Running the non-profit was just part of it, as was volunteering at the Castaway Café.

And today he was trying to erase his guilt by checking on his brother's ex-girlfriend.

He picked up flowers on his way, because everyone liked flowers, didn't they? But he went for tulips because it was spring, and because tulips felt more like an overture of friendship than any of the other bouquets on offer. The last thing he needed was Willow getting the wrong idea and giving him something else to feel guilty about.

He'd done a lot of work on his guilt issues, and he liked to think he'd come a long way. He knew it wasn't his fault his father had hated him but still felt socially obliged to support him as a son. He knew he hadn't imagined the bad feelings in his family dynamics, no matter how many people had lied and told him he was making it up, that his father loved both his sons equally.

He'd been almost twenty when he'd learned

the term 'gaslighting' but it had been the first step to changing his life.

This time, when he arrived at Willow's apartment building, he didn't use the code Ben had given him to gain entrance, but rang the buzzer instead. No answer.

Eli frowned. He should have called first, perhaps, but he didn't have her number. But if she wasn't here, he was just a guy standing in the street with a bunch of tulips looking hopeful about spring.

Just as he was debating what to do next, Willow appeared around the corner, weighed down with half a dozen shopping bags, and he relaxed into a smile. 'Let me help you with those.'

Willow blinked at him, then smiled cautiously. 'Eli. I didn't expect to see you again so soon.'

At least now the trauma of her panic attack had passed she'd managed to remember his name. She looked better too, like she might have actually slept since he saw her last.

Willow was always, always beautiful—at least, as far as he could tell from the photos he saw online or on billboards. But in her apartment that day she'd also looked…fragile.

Juggling bags with flowers, he nodded towards the tulips. 'I was bringing you these. An apology for the other day.'

'You really didn't have to.' Her smile tightened as she opened the door.

He followed her with the bags all the same. 'I wanted to.'

They took the elevator up to the apartment in awkward silence.

'Where do you want these?' Eli asked as they stepped inside.

Willow looked surprised, as if she'd forgotten he was carrying her shopping. 'Oh, just dump them by the door somewhere.'

Already there were more signs of habitation in the apartment than when he'd last visited—a sweater slung over the arm of a sofa, a book on the coffee table, coffee mugs on the kitchen counter. All of which reinforced his suspicion that the organisation of her apartment had happened in her absence.

'So, are you replacing things your home organisers decluttered for you?' he joked, gesturing towards the bags.

'What? Oh, no. I just...looked in the closet here and couldn't see anything I wanted to wear. So I went shopping.'

She said it airily, like a privileged woman used to replacing her entire wardrobe on a whim. But there was something in her eyes, something Eli recognised from people he'd worked with before. This wasn't a whim; it was a change.

Willow was making changes in her life. Was it in response to breaking up with Ben?

Eli knew from experience that change could be very positive—or it could be a distraction. Sometimes people changed everything about themselves outwardly, just to avoid dealing with the things that scared them within.

A breakup was a perfectly reasonable time for a makeover—he knew that from romcom movies he'd watched with ex-girlfriends.

So why did he feel like this was something more?

'Can I offer you a drink?' Willow flipped the kettle on, and Eli frowned. Had there even been a kettle in this kitchen the last time he was here? He only remembered the high-end coffee machine. 'Tea?'

'Uh, coffee, if that's okay,' he replied. Maybe Willow was getting back to her British roots after breaking up with her American boyfriend. That would make sense.

She nodded and reached for a jar, rather than the machine. When he frowned, she laughed self-deprecatingly. 'I never did figure out how to use that thing. But if you think you know, feel free!'

It didn't take long for him to make sense of the coffee machine—it wasn't very different to the one he had at home. Willow looked on, nodding politely and sipping her tea as he explained it to her. 'I can write it down, if you like…?'

'No, I'll…' She stopped and blushed prettily. 'Actually, that might be a good idea. Just in case.'

By the time he'd written down the instructions and she'd taped them to the front of the machine, ruining any aesthetic the designer and organiser had put in place for the kitchen, they were feeling more at ease with each other again.

'So, how are things going with your gala?' Willow folded her long legs under her on the corner of the sofa.

Eli, sitting across from her on the other sofa, reflected that this was far more comfortable than the floor. 'They're going.' His contacts had come through—the ones he'd been cultivating even as he'd waited for Ben to read the file he'd given him, knowing that his brother wasn't a sure thing. He didn't have the one big name sponsor he'd hoped Ben would provide, but he'd raised the money he needed through a few smaller ones with just a few phone calls. People wanted to be seen doing good in this city right now, and Eli was perfectly happy to take advantage of that. 'My team are still on the hunt for a few table sponsors, though, if you're interested?'

'How much?' Willow asked without blinking.

'Uh, five thousand dollars for a table of eight.'

'Can you take a credit card?' She was already reaching for her purse.

'You really want to help?' The words were out before he could stop them.

She hesitated. 'Why wouldn't I? I… I read up a bit on your work after you were here and, well, you're doing really important things. Helping the young people of New York City who really need that help.'

'Not all of them,' Eli admitted. 'There are too many that need the help. And a lot of other great organisations are doing just as much, and many are doing more.'

'But you're doing what you can,' Willow said firmly. 'Not many people do even that.'

'Well, if you're sure,' Eli said. Was this a good idea? Letting his brother's ex-girlfriend sponsor a table at his event? Making a connection between them—even an altruistic and charitable one—just as their relationship had ended?

Maybe not. But if he turned away a genuine donation for personal reasons...

'I'm sure.' Willow reached into her purse and pulled out a credit card. 'How do we do this?'

Rowan started to doubt the wisdom of her impulse almost as soon as Eli had picked up the phone to call the office so she could give Willow's credit card number to the fundraiser at the other end of the line. But she'd already had a personal spending spree on Willow's card—buying the sort of wardrobe that was Willow appropriate, but still felt a little bit like Rowan too. Now she wanted to do something more meaningful.

Willow had said she could spend as much as she wanted, on whatever mattered to her—and this mattered. Not just to her, but to lots of people.

She'd researched Eli and his non-profit organisation thoroughly after her call with Willow, and the more she'd read the more she'd been convinced that he was doing good work—and that his brother and her sister had barely even noticed. Ben probably hadn't even bothered to read that file Eli had been searching for the day they'd met.

She hadn't exactly *intended* to sponsor a table at his event or anything but, when the opportunity arose, it seemed like the obvious thing to do. The *right* thing. Given the way his face had lit up, he thought so too.

Eli handed his phone over to her with a smile. 'This is Sandra. She'll take you through the sponsorship form and take your donation, if you're still sure.'

Rowan nodded, and took the phone.

Sandra—a warm-sounding woman with a broad New York accent, the sort Rowan imagined from the movies—was funny, reassuring and made the whole process painless. Right up until the moment she asked, 'And can I take the names of the guests for your table?'

Of course, sponsoring a table meant filling it with people too. Why hadn't she realised that? It wasn't as if she could just call up Willow's friends and invite them to a gala dinner. She didn't even know who Willow's friends were these days, for a start.

'Uh, can I get back to you on that?'

'Sure, honey,' Sandra said. 'Just let me know when you know, yeah?'

A couple more questions and the call was done. Rowan handed the phone back to Eli and he had a few more words with Sandra before hanging up.

Then he turned to Rowan with a small frown line between his eyes. 'So, do you know who you're going to ask to join you at the dinner?'

Because of course *she'd* have to go too. God, she really hadn't thought this through at all, had she?

This was why she didn't usually make spur-of-the-moment decisions. They rarely ended well.

'Actually… I was wondering if *you'd* like to fill the table,' she said after a brief pause. 'I mean, there must be lots of people working behind the scenes at your non-profit who never get to attend the fancy fun stuff. Wouldn't you like to be able to reward them with a table at the dinner?'

There, that solved it! Eli could ask deserving volunteers and staff and she could just pay the money then stay the hell out of it.

'That would be…incredibly kind and thoughtful of you.' Eli was still frowning, despite his words. 'Are you sure?'

Rowan nodded fervently. 'Very.'

'Well, great!' Eli's expression cleared. 'There are definitely some long-time volunteers and staff who would love to be dressed up and enjoying the party rather than behind the scenes on the night—Sandra for one! And I'm sure they'll all enjoy having dinner with a celebrity like yourself.'

'Oh, I—' She broke off. How could she explain that she didn't want to actually attend without sounding like she was too superior to have dinner with the *staff*? 'That will be lovely,' she finished lamely.

So, apparently, she was going to need an evening gown too. Great.

'And since you're going to be there anyway...' Eli looked so hopeful, Rowan knew she wasn't going to like whatever came out of his mouth next. 'Perhaps you'd like to present some of our awards on the night?'

'Sure.' What else could she say, really? Although she was certain her smile must look fake.

'That's fantastic! Thank you, Willow.' Eli reached out and took her hand, his expression so earnest and sincere she couldn't even begin to look away. 'I can't tell you how much this will mean to everyone involved. It's not just the money—although we always appreciate that. It's you lending your name to the cause. It helps us raise the profile, get more people interested in our work, more people donating—everything. I know charity shouldn't require celebrities to get people's attention, but...' He shrugged.

'Sometimes it does,' Rowan finished for him, and he nodded.

She supposed that made sense, in a way. And she knew Willow was always very careful about what brands or causes she lent her name—or, more potently, her face—to for that very reason. People assumed that if she spoke about it, wore their brand or appeared at their events, then she endorsed everything about them. They were linked for ever.

Well, hopefully, her sister couldn't disapprove of supporting vulnerable teens in the city. Otherwise, Rowan was in for an earful the next time they spoke!

'I'm really glad to be able to help,' she said honestly. 'The work you're doing here... I wasn't just saying it when I said I know how much it matters. It's a cause that's...well. Close to my heart.'

She might have not been a teen runaway, or kicked out of her home by junkie parents, or struggling with mental health problems without access to the proper support. She was, in so many ways, hugely privileged and fortunate and she *knew* that.

But she also knew that if she and Willow hadn't looked the way they did, she might not have been.

The luck of the draw. Genetics shouldn't be something to be proud of, since she'd done nothing herself but be born with them.

Eli looked thoughtful. 'I wonder... How would you like to come down to the offices, and maybe one of our centres, and see the work we do up close? You can meet some of our staff before the dinner that way too.'

She should say no. She should be staying out of the way, only appearing as Willow when strictly necessary. The more people she interacted with, the more chance there was of giving herself away. Of people realising she wasn't Willow at all. And she couldn't risk that, for her sister's sake.

Especially with Ben's brother.

But, all the same, she found herself saying, 'That would be lovely,' and a warm feeling spread through her at Eli's smile.

CHAPTER FOUR

THE FOLLOWING FRIDAY, Eli led Willow into the main offices of Launch through the back door that led to the administrative centre, feeling unexpectedly apprehensive about the whole thing, considering it had been his idea in the first place.

He wasn't even entirely sure why. Willow had been nothing but gracious and generous and—above all—*interested* in the non-profit company he ran, ever since that day in her apartment. But being philanthropic from a distance was one thing, Eli knew. It was easy to throw money at a problem so you didn't have to look at it.

He hadn't expected Ben's ex-girlfriend to show any interest at all in his foundation or the work they did. Most of the people in Ben's circle that he met paid lip service to caring about kids or society's problems, but they didn't get involved. He'd assumed Willow would be the same. But she kept surprising him. She seemed so unlike the media image of her he'd thought he knew, it was hard to remember that she was the same woman who'd hung adoringly on Ben's arm for the last two years.

For starters, she seemed genuinely interested in Launch. He just hoped that interest would outlast a meeting with reality.

From the way she was looking around her curiously as they entered the building, he suspected it would. So what was he really worried about?

Maybe it was because Ben was back in the city. He'd called Eli the night before about an upcoming report due out from the family business. Ben might be the CEO, but Eli was also a stakeholder, so still technically involved. His income from his seat on the board of directors was what had made it possible for him to set up Launch in the first place.

Eli hadn't mentioned Willow when they'd talked. He was still busy pretending to himself that he didn't know why that was.

It wasn't as if they were doing anything wrong. He just...didn't want to have to explain his sudden acquaintance with his brother's ex to Ben.

'So how much work do you actually do here?' Willow asked as they waited for her visitor pass to be printed at reception.

He looked at her in surprise. 'Uh, this is my job. Full-time. So I'm here most days. It's not...it's not like a figurehead position or anything.'

She smiled softly. 'That's not what I meant. I wasn't doubting your commitment to the cause, Eli.'

Behind the reception desk, Addison gave him a cheeky grin as she handed over Willow's pass. Reaching out, he hung the lanyard over Willow's neck as she ducked her head to make it easier for him.

Addison was making hearts with her hands and batting her eyelashes at them. Eli turned Willow towards the elevators before she noticed.

Sending Addison a warning look over his shoulder, he asked Willow, 'So what did you mean?'

'Just that I assume things like the shelters and such are off site? Is this building just for administration, or what?' She stepped into the elevator and he followed, pressing the buttons to take them up to the top floor. They could work downwards, he figured.

'This building houses the helpline staff, the fundraising staff, the admin staff—and through the other entrance on the ground floor we have the Castaway Café, which is actually quite often kids' first port of call with us. I'll show you that later; we can have a coffee.'

'That sounds good.' The elevator surged upwards. 'So, where do we start?'

'My office, of course,' Eli replied.

When he'd been looking for a headquarters, location had been key. Ben had tried to convince him to look at buildings near the company HQ, but Eli had refused. They needed to be somewhere close to the kids he wanted to serve, so that meant moving out of the areas of Manhattan he'd grown up in, and towards the ones that needed his help.

The building he'd chosen, sandwiched between a laundrette and a Malaysian takeaway, had needed a lot of work. But it gave them three floors, kitchen facilities on the first floor for the café he'd envisioned, space for a decent phone bank, and good open-plan offices for the rest of the staff. They'd done up the inside to freshen it up and make it feel new, but left the façade so it matched the surroundings. They didn't want to stand out—not for how they looked, anyway.

Eli wanted their work to stand out for them.

The elevator doors opened, and Eli let Willow step out first, right into the hustle and bustle of the office floor. A few people looked up—one or two even did a double-take, Eli noted with amusement—but they didn't let their latest arrival disturb their work.

The whole floor was buzzing with activity and a feeling of purpose. Eli felt the warmth of pride in his chest as Willow surveyed the scene and smiled.

Then she turned to him. 'Where's your office?'

'This way.'

He introduced her to a few people as they passed their desks, and she asked interested and insightful questions about what they were doing—without getting into the kind of details that were confidential. Eventually, they reached the far corner of the floor, diagonally opposite and as far from the elevator as possible.

'And this is me.' He gestured towards the L-shaped desk with its overflowing in-tray, monitor and laptop stand, and a poster on the wall featuring a quote that read: 'Never doubt that a small group of thoughtful, committed citizens can change the world; indeed, it's the only thing that ever has'.

'Isn't that from the TV show, *The West Wing*?' Willow asked, looking at it.

'It was actually the anthropologist Margaret Mead who said it first,' Eli replied. 'But I had to look that up after watching the episode.'

'Fair enough.' She stared out of the window behind his desk for a long moment, then turned around to look back over the open-plan office. 'You didn't want an office with a door and a view?'

'I have a view,' he pointed out, nodding towards the window.

'You don't face it, though. You face your staff.' He shrugged, and she continued. 'And you're as far away from the lift as it's possible to get, so you have to walk through and see every one of them on your way.'

'I like to be involved.'

'I'm seeing that.' She looked up at him, and this time her smile was considering, thoughtful—and he couldn't look away from it.

At least until the whirlwind that was his assistant, Kelly, came racing across the office from wherever she'd been, doing whatever she'd been doing.

'Eli! I *can't* come to the gala, I just can't!' Kelly's hands were clenched in fists at her sides, and he got the impression that she'd been waiting to tell him this for some time, and working herself up about it.

'That's a shame, Kelly,' he said calmly. 'It would have been lovely to have you there, after all the work you've put in to make it happen.'

'Well, I can't.' Her lower lip was trembling.

'That's fine,' he said. 'It's no problem. But… can I ask why?'

Now tears sprang into her eyes—but it seemed to him they were more angry tears than sad ones. 'Because not all of us look like Miss Supermodel here!' she snapped, waving a hand towards Willow. 'There isn't a dress in New York City that will fit over these hips without making me look like a sackful of potatoes.'

Eli's jaw clenched. He'd never spent any time thinking about his assistant's hips. Mostly, he thought about how she always had the file he needed ready before he needed it, how she cared deeply about the work they were doing and always gave everything she had to getting things done right.

He hated that something as stupid as a dress might stop her celebrating everything she'd worked so hard for.

Tears glistened on Kelly's cheeks as she glanced up at Willow from under her eyelashes. 'No offence meant. I mean, it was very nice of you to offer us the table. Only I'd stick out like a sore thumb at something like that. But that's not your fault. Sorry.'

Eli looked over to see if Willow was offended, but she seemed more thoughtful than angry.

'No, no, I totally understand,' Willow said, smiling graciously. 'Actually, uh, I might be able to help you with that.'

Help?

Just when he thought she was done surprising him.

Rowan regretted it almost the instant the words were out of her mouth.

This wasn't something Willow would do. This was a *Rowan* thing, and it was exactly how she was going to get caught out in her deception and let Willow down.

In fact, this was *just* how it had happened

with that woman and her daughter outside the dress shop. She hated to see someone upset by something as basic as *clothes*. Hated for anyone to feel ostracised by style or fashion. Not when she could do something about it.

So maybe she didn't regret it all that much. Except for the way Eli was looking at her right now.

'You can help?' he asked, sounding sceptical. 'How? You have…connections, I suppose?'

'I do.' Or, well, Willow did. 'But actually…' She gave Kelly an apologetic look. 'Most of the designers I knew—know—only do sample sizing.'

'Exactly!' Kelly said, vindicated. 'They don't want people like me wearing their clothes!'

'But I *do* have some…experience *making* dresses,' Rowan said quickly. 'My, uh, my sister is a designer, as it happens, and she taught me a lot. If I can get your measurements and some ideas of what sort of a dress you're looking for, I can bring some fabrics in for you to look at, and some draft designs? What do you think?'

Kelly was staring at her in shock. So was Eli, come to that. This *really* wasn't the sort

of thing Willow would have done. But actually…neither of them really knew Willow, so
how could they be sure?

And she wanted to help. This whole organisation was doing so much good for the young
people of the city. If she could help *them*, just
a tiny bit…why wouldn't she?

'You *make* dresses?' Kelly asked. 'Seriously? When people must just *give* them to
you all the time?'

'Well, it's my sister who's really great at
it,' Rowan said. 'But I know enough to make
you look good, I promise.'

'It really would be a shame for you to miss
the gala,' Eli added persuasively.

Kelly looked between them for a moment,
then nodded. 'Okay. We'll try it. How do we
start?'

Rowan beamed, then glanced up at Eli.
'Can we use your desk?'

'Go ahead. It's not like I'm going to get any
work done this morning, anyway. I'll fetch
the coffees, shall I?' He shot a grin at Kelly,
who seemed pleased at this turnabout in their
relationship.

'That would be wonderful.' Rowan pulled
a notebook from her bag, grabbed a pen and

dropped into Eli's desk chair. 'So, what sort of a dress were you thinking of?'

Out of the corner of her eye, she was vaguely aware of Eli watching them and shaking his head, before he went to find the promised coffee. She suspected that there would be a conversation later about this. That he wasn't fully convinced—or at least that he knew something was off.

She'd have to figure out how to deal with that. How to keep lying to him, even as they spent more time together.

This wasn't part of the plan she and Willow had hammered out at her kitchen table in Rumbelow. She wasn't supposed to get close to Eli—she wasn't supposed to get close to *anyone,* least of all Ben's brother.

But it had happened anyway, and she couldn't bring herself to regret it. Not when she was sitting here contributing a very small amount to the work his non-profit was doing—even if only by making his assistant's life a little brighter.

It took some coaxing to get Kelly to tell her the sort of dress she *really* wanted to wear—rather than the sort of dress she *thought* she should wear, at her size.

'It should be black, right?' Kelly said anxiously. 'Black is slimming.'

'Black can be elegant and classic,' Rowan said evenly. 'But if it doesn't really feel like you, that doesn't matter. Other colours can be those things too.'

Kelly sighed. 'I just don't want to look huge and awful.'

Rowan took her hand across the desk. 'I promise you that you won't. You're a beautiful woman, and we're going to create a dress for you that shows that to the world. That makes you feel like your very best you. Okay?'

It was a speech she'd given to girls and women back home a hundred times over the past few years. Girls who thought they were too fat for prom, or that they couldn't wear a classic strapless prom dress because they were 'flat as a board' and had nothing to hold it up. Students who didn't feel at ease in either a traditional prom dress or a tuxedo, and wanted something new, something different—something that felt like them. Women who needed something to wear to an ex's wedding and wanted it to make them feel incredible while also not looking like they were trying too hard.

Finding a dress to match how a person wanted to feel while wearing it? That was Rowan's speciality, and she knew she could do it for Kelly too.

By the time they'd drunk the coffee Eli returned with, Rowan had a page full of notes of Kelly's likes, dislikes, wishes and dreams and fears for her dress—and the start of a picture growing in her mind.

She smiled at Eli's assistant as she closed her notebook. 'Well, I can definitely work with this.'

Kelly's expression grew anxious as her gaze flitted between Rowan and Eli. 'It's kind of you to listen to me chatter about this stuff. But I really can't afford a bespoke dress—or even the fabric for one. He doesn't pay us *that* much, you know!'

Rowan shook her head. 'This one's on me, Kelly. Just call it an extra donation to the cause.'

Her cause, of helping women feel confident when people were staring, like themselves even when they were dressed up, and like they deserved beautiful things.

They made their goodbyes, Kelly thanking Rowan profusely as they left, tears sparkling in her eyes.

'That was kind of you,' Eli murmured, one hand against the small of her back as he guided her to the lift.

Rowan shrugged. 'Why not be kind, when we can?'

'An excellent question,' Eli replied. But Rowan couldn't help but notice the way he looked at her as they stepped into the lift. As if she were a puzzle he hadn't quite figured out—but fully intended to.

And soon.

Eli wasn't by nature a suspicious man. He liked to believe the best of people, until they proved otherwise. But Rowan had all his senses on high alert.

The most ridiculous part was that she'd done it by being kind, generous and thoughtful to a fault. Her crimes, such as they were, boiled down to donating to a cause he believed passionately in, helping a woman he was fond of, and now engaging with the kids who found sanctuary at the Castaway Café.

'She seems to really get them.' Standing beside him by the counter, the café manager, Sven, shook his head. 'I wouldn't have expected it from someone like her.'

'Me neither,' Eli agreed softly, watching as

Willow drew some of the youths at the table into conversation, asking a question about their hopes for the future, rather than the life they'd run away from.

And that was what it came down to in the end, wasn't it? His own prejudices and preconceptions getting in the way of the reality he observed.

He'd never got to know Willow when she was dating Ben—he'd never had the chance. He'd assumed she had no interest in meeting her boyfriend's less commercially successful brother. He knew he didn't move in the same circles or worlds that Ben and Willow did, because he didn't *want* to. That had been a conscious choice when he'd gained his inheritance at the tender age of twenty-one.

He hadn't wanted to live in that superficial world of celebrity and fame for fame's sake. He'd wanted to do something more than be photographed partying on yachts. It hadn't been a popular decision—with his friends, his brother or his girlfriend at the time.

But he'd done it anyway. And he'd never regretted it.

So he'd assumed, based on the reactions of others, that Willow—who he'd never met and certainly didn't know outside the celebrity gossip pages—felt the same. That was on him.

Why *hadn't* they got to know each other better before now, then? Lack of opportunity? Given how interested Willow was in the work of Launch and the Castaway Café now, he couldn't believe it was because she hadn't wanted to know more. Had she even known what he did for a living? Had Ben spoken about him at all?

Ben. Whichever way he looked at it, it seemed that Ben must have been the one keeping them apart. Why? Because he was ashamed of him?

It was a possibility. Eli wondered what he'd think about their meeting now—and working together, sort of. How he'd feel about Willow getting involved with Launch. Could this be some sort of bizarre revenge scheme she was planning against his brother? He couldn't see how.

But as for what Ben would think… There was no reason for his brother to be concerned. This was a purely professional arrangement, and Ben and Willow weren't even together any more—well, not at the moment, anyway. Eli wouldn't let this evolve into anything that could embarrass his brother or the company in any way. So really, why should Ben care?

And why was Eli so sure he would?

He turned the idea over in his head once or twice, then tucked it away for thinking about later.

Right now, he was focused on Willow.

Willow, who was now being shown around the café, admiring the wall art—created by some of the regulars, in a mix of styles. They had the graffiti wall, the cartoon and manga wall and also some framed sketches and even watercolours on the last wall from an art course they'd run in one of the back rooms a few months ago.

He'd never seen the kids react to someone new like this. She'd got their emotional barriers down in record time, and seemed to genuinely connect with them. How did she do it? And what was it in her past that made her understand them?

Every one of these kids had difficult—often impossible—relationships with their families. Maybe they'd been kicked out, or perhaps they were trying to work through their problems with the help of Launch's trained counsellors. But, as far as Eli knew, Willow didn't have any estranged family in her past. She'd sounded genuinely fond when talking of her sister, for instance.

Her sister. Maybe that was the in.

Whatever it was, he wanted to know more.

Because he just couldn't shake the feeling, unfair as it might be, that this was all an act, somehow. That Willow was hiding something—a secret that would make sense of all the things he didn't yet understand.

He hated not knowing secrets. All those years of sensing people were whispering to each other as they looked at him, but not knowing what they were saying. These days, he just asked them outright.

Which was what he should do with Willow. Maybe over dinner.

No, not dinner.

Except why not? A *working* dinner. A client dinner, like he had hundreds of times a year, persuading people who could make a difference to make a difference at his foundation. That was all.

Nobody, not even Ben, could object to that.

Willow bounced away from the pack of kids, smiling, and made her way over to him.

'This place is brilliant,' she said. 'I can see how at home they all are here. You've given

them what they really needed—a place to belong.'

'That was the idea,' Eli admitted. 'I didn't...
I didn't always feel at home or like I belonged,
growing up. And my experience was definitely at the top, most privileged end of that
emotion. So, I guess I wanted to give more
to the kids who need it now.'

Give a truth to get a truth, that was how
it worked, right? He'd opened up, given her
an insight into his own past, so maybe she'd
share something of hers—if not now, then
soon.

He'd half-expected her to ask about Ben,
and how he fitted into that vision of Eli's
childhood. But apparently that thought didn't
occur to her as she moved breezily on.

'The artwork is fantastic too. There's some
real talent there. But, more importantly,
they're so *proud* that someone admired their
work enough to display it. That really means
something to them.' She smiled up at him. 'I
love this place.'

He couldn't help but smile back. 'I'm glad.
Actually, I was wondering...would you like to
get dinner with me tonight? We could talk some
more about the work we do here, and maybe
how you could be involved longer term?'

Her face started to fall, and he hurried on. 'Only if you wanted to be, of course. I just… You seemed to have a real connection with these kids, and—'

'No, no! I would… I would like that.' Her smile said otherwise, though, wobbling a little as she continued. 'Pick me up at eight?'

Eli nodded. 'Will do.' And then he'd figure out what secrets Willow was keeping from him—one way or another.

CHAPTER FIVE

ROWAN HADN'T REALLY thought that anyone drove in Manhattan, but Eli did. When Willow went places with Ben she knew he had a driver, but his brother seemed to prefer to do the work himself. He picked her up at eight on the dot and, after a moment of staring silently at her, had driven them to the restaurant he'd chosen.

It was the dress that made him stare, Rowan knew that. Not the fact that she was in it.

Her shopping spree had mostly included clothes for wearing around the apartment, or for running errands in the city. She hadn't really envisioned fancy meals out at that point. So she'd had to raid Willow's wardrobe for something suitable.

And Willow's wardrobe was full of possibilities for a woman wanting to stand out and be looked at. Not so many for a woman wanting to blend in and pass people by.

She'd chosen the least flashy option—a midi-length, fire-engine-red dress that was cut high in the front but very low over her back, and flared out around her thighs—paired it with the only pair of Willow's shoes she thought she could walk in, kept her make-up and jewellery simple, and hoped for the best.

The best being not falling over in someone else's meal because the black heels were still too high.

Oh. And not being outed as not Willow. That would be good too.

She'd had second, third and fourth thoughts about this dinner while she was getting ready. She'd even called the real Willow and asked for advice on how to get out of it.

But her sister had been so excited that Rowan had met someone and was going out for a fancy dinner, she hadn't seemed to care who it was—or let Rowan get a word in to warn her.

'That's exactly *the sort of thing I'd do— go out for dinner with a handsome man. I mean—he is handsome, right? But yes, you should definitely go. Because I guarantee Ben will have been off being seen with some other woman while we're broken up, so I should too. This is perfect.'*

By that point, it seemed too late to tell her that the man in question was Ben's brother.

Or that it was a working dinner, not an actual date.

Willow had rung off, and Rowan had sighed and put on the dress. And now, here she was.

The restaurant Eli had chosen was thankfully small, not too busy and smelled delicious. Rowan breathed a sigh of relief as she took her seat at the back of the room. From what she knew of Ben, this was the last place he would be seen, which meant that the chances of bumping into him tonight were slim. Willow might have wanted her to be somewhere more high profile, somewhere she might get photographed to prove she was in New York not Cornwall, but this suited Rowan just fine.

'I hope you like Italian,' Eli said as they were handed their menus.

'It's my favourite,' she assured him. 'And the best thing is, in this dress, when I spill spaghetti sauce down me you won't even be able to see it!'

That surprised a laugh from him. 'I wasn't sure if, with your career, carbs were off-limits or something.'

They probably should be, if she wanted to

really seem like Willow. But Italian really *was* her favourite. And the restaurant was quiet. Who'd know?

'A well-balanced diet includes all the food groups, as far as possible,' she said instead. Hard-won knowledge she'd had to learn *after* she'd left modelling, but it was still true.

'That's what I always think.' Eli relaxed into his chair. 'Tiramisu is a food group, right?'

'Definitely,' Rowan agreed fervently.

They made easy conversation over menu choices and a glass of wine, and it wasn't until they'd finished their main course that the discussion turned to areas Rowan knew she had to be completely on guard with.

'So, growing up famous must have been weird?' Eli swirled the last of his red wine around his glass before swallowing it. He'd only had the one—and had already ordered a coffee with dessert—because he was driving. She'd also only had one because she didn't want any secrets to slip out if she got even the tiniest bit tipsy.

'I guess…when it's all you know, you don't always realise how weird it is,' she said carefully. 'Like you growing up rich, I suppose.'

'I suppose,' Eli agreed. 'Except… I still went to school and college, did all the usual things a kid was supposed to do. My father just paid more for it.' There was a note in his voice she couldn't place. Not resentment—Eli had been nothing but grateful for his good fortune in life in every conversation they'd had. But maybe…a longing? For something else? She wasn't sure.

'I went to school too, for a while,' Rowan said with a slight shrug. 'We moved around a bit when I was younger, but by my teenage years we were settled in London, and we just flew out for shoots and shows. It was weird going from the classroom to the catwalk and back again, though.'

'I imagine it would be.' Eli pushed his empty glass aside, and leaned his elbows on the table. 'Then after school you moved to New York?'

After school I was a mess, and barely talking to my family, and on all kinds of anxiety drugs my mother convinced the doctor to give me, just counting the days until I could run away.

'We split our time between London and New York,' she said, because it sounded better than 'it didn't really matter where we lived, because I was holed up in my room whenever I wasn't needed to be in front of a camera or an audience'.

'Is your mother still in London?'

Rowan shook her head, using the arrival of the tiramisu and coffees they'd ordered as an excuse to look away from his searching eyes. Her mother was *definitely* not a subject she wanted to get into with him.

'LA,' she answered shortly. 'She got remarried, to an actor.'

'Do you see her often?' Eli pressed. No, not pressed. This was perfectly normal first date conversation. He was just being polite.

Not that this was a date at all, she reminded her brain sharply. As far as Eli was concerned, she was his brother's on-again off-again girlfriend. And she already knew enough about Eli to know he'd never make a move on his brother's girl.

Which was weird in itself. She *didn't* know Eli, not really—and neither did Willow. But she felt as if she did.

He'd been nothing but respectful of her since they'd met, and that slightly stunned look when he'd picked her up was the only hint that he even found her attractive at all. And Rowan knew better than most that external attractiveness meant next to nothing when it came to happiness.

No, Eli had shown no interest in her beyond what she could do for his foundation, and a few polite questions about her life as a model. That was all.

Asking about a person's mother was perfectly normal. It was Rowan's relationship with her mother that wasn't.

She thought back to her last conversation with Willow about their mother. Her twin tended to avoid the subject with her, for obvious reasons, but every now and then it came up anyway. What had she said?

'Uh…sometimes we get together if I'm working out there. But you know how life gets. So busy for everyone these days.' Rowan dug into her tiramisu with gusto, hoping that if her mouth was filled with creamy coffee dessert she couldn't be expected to answer too many more questions.

'What about your sister?' Eli asked. 'The one who taught you how to make dresses. Didn't she used to model with you? Yeah, there's that famous photo of the two of you together. What happened there? Are you still close?'

Oh, this was even dodgier ground, and Rowan really wasn't sure how to handle it.

'She used to, but she decided it wasn't for her.' She gave a light, inconsequential shrug that hopefully covered the full story without having to give any details. 'She lives in Cornwall, in England now. I don't get to visit often, but we talk on the phone a lot.'

'Hmm.' His tiramisu bowl empty, Eli leaned back in his seat and studied her. Rowan tried hard not to flinch under his gaze.

'How about you and *your* brother?' She flung the question back defensively, before realising she should already know the full story about them from Ben. 'I mean, isn't it strange that we never really got to know each other when Ben and I were still dating?'

'Yes,' Eli said, as if the word meant more than it did. 'It is.'

Rowan turned her attention back to her tiramisu and prayed for the evening to be over soon.

Just the thought sent disappointment cascading through her. Because until he'd started asking awkward questions, she'd been enjoying herself far more than she should have been, under the circumstances.

This was supposed to be business. At best, a charade for Willow's benefit. She should want to get home, forget about Eli and get on with acting like Willow. Not hanging out with her sister's ex's brother and getting involved

in charity work she had no place getting involved in—especially when she knew she'd
be leaving soon and, without Willow's money,
wouldn't be able to support them anyway.

She should be grateful to get out of this en-
counter without giving anything away. And
she should make damn sure not to get herself
into such a risky position again.

So that was what she'd do. Definitely.

Except, as they left the restaurant and Eli
placed the palm of his hand on the small of
her bare back to guide her out, she shivered at
his touch. The kind of shiver that betrayed all
her protestations that this was just business,
that she was just playing a part, that she was
only trying to help out a good cause.

The kind of shiver that told her how much
more she wanted here.

Oh, hell. She was in trouble now.

Dinner with Willow had been…disconcert-
ing. That was the only word Eli had for it.

Even asking her in the first place had probably been a mistake, but something about her
seemed to make him act impulsively—which
was not a good thing.

Almost as soon as he'd invited her, the
doubts and worries had started flooding in.

Yes, he wanted to know her secrets—but what if she got annoyed with his questions and pulled out of the gala? Or told Ben he'd been bothering her? What if Ben saw them in the restaurant? Or heard they'd been seen by someone else? How would that make him feel? Eli knew he'd hate it if Ben was seen with a woman he'd just broken up with—and probably planned to get back together with—however innocent the occasion.

But he'd invited her now. And he *did* want answers. So he'd tried to mitigate the risks by booking his favourite cosy Italian, where no one from Ben's circle would ever be seen dead—only realising too late the romantic vibes it gave off.

And then there was the dress Willow wore. From the front, it looked positively modest, with its high neck and the low hem, but the fire-engine-red colour should have been a warning sign. When she turned around to put her jacket on, the back on the damn thing dipped all the way to the base of her spine, revealing acres of smooth, bare flesh that just begged to be touched.

But he couldn't touch it. Because she was his brother's girlfriend—at least some of the time. And Eli would not be that man. There was a line, and he couldn't cross it.

Besides, they might not be together right now, but Eli knew Ben. He would be expecting Willow to be waiting for him whenever he decided it was time for them to get back together. Ben wasn't used to the world making decisions without him. In Ben's world, everything waited for him to decide.

And if he decided that he wanted Willow back, it was hard to imagine her resisting. After all, she'd gone back to him the last half dozen times, hadn't she?

Eli didn't understand their relationship. He hadn't understood it before either, but now he'd spent some time with Willow it made even less sense.

Willow cared about things, deeply. She connected with other people, she wanted to help, to be involved in people's lives. And Ben...

Eli tried not to think bad things about his older brother. But that didn't mean he couldn't see the influence their upbringing had had on him. All the ways Ben took after their father.

Where Eli had been the black sheep, the red-headed stepchild, Ben had been the golden boy. The son and heir. Their father's firstborn—and possibly only born, if you listened to the rumours.

And Mack O'Donnell had leaned into that.

He'd paraded Ben around his business associates from the moment he was old enough to wear a suit, making sure they all knew this was the future of the company, right there in a tiny waistcoat. He'd drilled Ben on facts and figures, on strategy and management techniques.

He'd showered him with expectation and information—but not necessarily with love. Mack O'Donnell hadn't been that kind of man.

Of course, Eli hadn't had the love either, but he also hadn't had all the pressure and expectation. Maybe that was what made the difference. Eli never felt as if he had to live up to their father's example, or memory. Ben did.

Eli hadn't seen Ben and Willow together often, but from what he had seen, and from what his brother had said about the relationship, he'd always got the impression that it was more of a convenient arrangement than true love. Oh, he was sure they liked each other well enough, and of course Willow was beautiful, and Ben was handsome, so they looked *right* together…but it had never seemed like the sort of relationship Eli would have wanted for himself. Apart from anything else, if Eli loved a woman, he'd be faithful to her. And there was no way he'd be taking any other women out on yachts, or to parties or dinner, the way Ben always did when they were split up—and sometimes even when they were still together.

He'd felt sorry for his brother, settling for a businesslike arrangement that fitted what the media *thought* a relationship should look like for a supermodel and a CEO, rather than holding out for the real thing.

Eli had never found the real thing either, despite his best efforts, but he had faith it was out there somewhere. Ben didn't even seem to be looking.

But now he'd met Willow, spent time with her, got to know her…it all made even less sense.

He could understand, almost, Ben settling for a relationship like that. But why would *Willow?* When she was a woman so clearly open and ready for so much more?

With someone like me.

No. Not with him. He was the *last* person who could consider dating Willow.

Something he should have remembered before he'd put his hand on the bare skin at the base of her spine last night to guide her out of the restaurant, before she'd put her jacket back on.

Just *touching* her had sent his mind into a spin—and driven all suspicious thoughts about her from it. Until he'd woken up this morning and remembered how incompletely she'd answered his questions. Nothing she'd told him had explained her affinity for kids estranged from their families, or her sudden interest in supporting Launch.

Something was going on with her.

And I need to figure out what it is before I let her get any more involved in my non-profit. Or my life.

And without his brother noticing. Because either Ben would think Eli was making a move on her, or that he didn't trust her, and neither option would end well.

He headed into the next week with that determination in mind, making a conscious effort not to visit Willow's apartment, and leaving communication about the gala to Kelly.

Which was working well until, on Wednesday, he arrived at the office around lunchtime, after a morning of working at home, to discover that his desk had already been taken over by pages of sketches and strips of material.

'Sorry, boss,' Kelly said. 'People were using the conference room, and your desk was the next biggest space. Apart from the café tables downstairs at the Castaway, and we didn't want to risk getting juice or anything on these gorgeous fabrics.' She hugged a gold, shiny one to her chest.

Willow, standing behind his desk, gave him an apologetic smile. 'We won't be long. I think we're nearly there.'

'Then maybe we could grab lunch? Since you're here.' Damn, he hadn't meant to say that. So much for keeping his distance. But seeing her there, her blonde hair bundled up on the back of her head in a clip, her lip between her teeth as she concentrated on what Kelly was saying…how was he supposed to resist that?

He needed to, though. Somehow.

She glanced up again, that same, slightly guilty look on her face. 'Ah, we might be a *little* bit longer than that.'

Eli sighed, even though actually it was with relief. Another intimate, private meal with Willow might be his undoing. 'Well, I guess I'd better go pick up takeout for us then, hadn't I?'

She beamed at that, and the warm feeling it gave him was enough to reignite all the worries he'd had at dinner—at least until Kelly thrust the lunch order clipboard into his hands, and the rest of the office started giving him their orders too.

Rowan laughed as she watched Eli make his way to the lift, a full sheet of lunch orders clutched in his hands. 'You certainly all have a very informal way of working with the boss here.'

Kelly nodded, tilting her head slightly as she studied her. 'I guess it's kind of different at his brother's office, huh?'

Rowan froze, realising the position she'd inadvertently put herself in here. *Of course* Eli's staff were interested in the woman he was spending time with—especially since she was his brother's ex-girlfriend. *Of course* they'd want to know more.

And of course she didn't *know* more. She'd never even *met* Ben.

Oh, she was treading some very treacherous waters here, just spending time with Eli. She knew that—that was why she'd tried to

stay away from him since their dinner together. And yet she couldn't seem to stop herself stepping into his world.

'Uh, yeah,' she hedged, since Kelly was
still waiting for an answer about Ben's office.
'You know, all very serious business.'

'I'm sure,' Kelly replied, obviously waiting
for her to say more.

She didn't.

Instead, she tried to draw Kelly's attention back to the choices they needed to make
about fabric and design. But other members
of staff were drawing close now too, questions in their gazes.

'We've never actually met Eli's brother,'
one of them said.

'Yeah, he wouldn't deign to come here,'
another added.

'But we all know what we've heard,' Kelly
said, and the staff around her nodded.

This was the father of her sister's child. She
shouldn't be gossiping about him with people
who'd never met him. But at the same time…
she needed an outsider's perspective, and it
hardly seemed likely that Eli was going to
discuss his brother with her—not when he
still believed they'd been dating until a week
or two ago.

Yet it was a risk. If they told Eli, or it got back to Ben…or worse, she could blow her cover completely. She was already acting too un-Willow-like. Especially with Eli. But she had to know what Willow had got herself into.

So she took a breath and asked, 'What have you heard?'

A lot, seemed to be the answer.

It was hard to get it all straight, with everyone eager to add to the conversation. *They* at least didn't seem concerned about badmouthing a man to his ex—probably because she *was* his ex, and they figured that had to be for a reason.

But the crux of their issues seemed to be with Ben's lack of interest in Launch, their work and his brother in general.

'Took me three weeks to even get him on the phone for Eli to talk about the gala,' Kelly said. 'That snooty secretary of his kept telling me he was "far too busy to be bothered". Bothered! By his own brother!'

'You weren't here when he *did* get him on the phone, though,' another woman said— Rowan thought it was the same Sandra who'd taken her sponsorship money on the phone.

'What happened?' Rowan asked curiously.

'Well, Eli was just trying to tell him about the gala, and the sponsorship, and how this year he's trying to make it a real spectacle— bigger than ever before—and how he wanted the family name blazoned across everything as the main sponsor.' Sandra glanced around to make sure Eli wasn't returning before she continued. 'But his brother wasn't listening. Kept talking about how the company already did plenty of high-profile charity work, that it didn't need to start associating with the dregs of society too.'

A gasp went around at that. Rowan wasn't surprised. She felt her own jaw tighten at the description of the kids Eli and his team were trying to help.

'And then Eli asked if he could at least drop off some information about the event, and the work we were raising money for, and Ben finally agreed,' Sandra finished. 'But I don't know what happened to it, because he sure as hell hasn't forked out any money for the cause.'

'No. He didn't,' Rowan said thoughtfully.

Instead, Ben had abandoned the file, probably unread, in Willow's apartment, and gone off on a yacht with his latest flame, according to the gossip websites. Rowan hoped Willow wasn't reading them, back home in Rumbelow.

'I'm sure there must be something good about the man,' Kelly went on, shaking her head. 'I mean, you dated him, honey, and *you* seem perfectly lovely! But the way he treats his brother…he sure makes it hard to see it. You know?'

'I know,' Rowan said with feeling.

She needed to call Willow tonight. Find out if there was more to why she was hiding out in her cottage, while Rowan paraded around New York pretending to be her, than she'd originally thought.

Because if Ben treated Willow the way he apparently treated Eli… Rowan wasn't surprised she didn't want to bring up a child with him as the father. Because why would he treat a child any differently than grown people?

Ben seemed the sort to ride roughshod over everyone, without listening or considering what they wanted or needed. Rowan had grown up with a person like that as her mother.

She wouldn't wish it on anyone. Let alone her own nephew or niece.

CHAPTER SIX

'LUNCH IS SERVED!' Eli strolled into the office, laden with food, to find almost his entire staff gathered around his desk—and around Willow.

Oh, good. Because that wasn't suspicious— or alarming—at all.

Eli knew he'd built a good team here—a family, almost. And he wasn't surprised they were all interested in the new woman in his life, even if she was only there because she was his brother's ex-girlfriend. Even if there could never be more between them.

Kelly wouldn't see that. Or Sandra. They were romantics, at heart.

Maybe they all were, really. Thinking they could change the world. What was more romantic than that?

People scattered with their sandwiches as he handed them out, and he was actually allowed to sit at his desk finally and check his emails— although his focus was shot because Willow was sitting opposite him, making notes in her notebook, a stack of sketches and fabric teetering beside her, as she nibbled at her lunch.

More than once, Eli thought he was composing a response to an email, only to discover that he was actually just watching Willow, thinking how different she was to the woman he'd expected. Willow, who was sitting there oblivious to him. Just being… beautiful and adorable and absorbed in doing something nice for someone else…and still his brother's ex-girlfriend.

He'd actually spoken to Ben the night before—an unusual occurrence in itself, more so when his brother was off on his boat, enjoying himself. Apparently, there was a board meeting being scheduled in the next few weeks—there'd be an email coming out— but Eli shouldn't worry about being there. Ben knew he had a lot on with the upcoming gala, and all the follow-up that would entail, and didn't want him to overload himself trying to do both when the meeting would just be a boring routine one.

Hearing his brother's concern about his workload, and the fact that he'd remembered the gala at all, had only made Eli feel more guilty about his dreams the night before. Because of course they'd been about Willow. Willow in that fire-engine-red dress with no back, looking over her shoulder at him as she slipped the straps down her arms and let it fall to the ground...

God, he was a terrible person. He'd even let the memory of the dream run in his mind for a moment or two, until Ben said, 'Hey, did you get that file from her apartment, by the way? Do you know if she's back in the country? I think she's ignoring my calls, unless our time zones are completely out of whack.'

Eli had started so violently he'd almost knocked over his drink. 'Uh, she's back in New York, I think.' *I know.* 'I bumped into her when I was picking up the file. She, uh, actually came on board to sponsor a table at the gala.'

Ben just laughed at that. 'That's a new one in her repertoire for making me feel guilty when we're apart! Well, good. At least one of us is getting something out of this current separation. Just keep an eye on her for me, will you? I don't want her doing anything stupid that means we can't get back together again next time one of us needs the PR boost.'

Keep an eye on her. Well, yeah, he could definitely do that.

But now, watching Willow eat a chicken salad wrap, and frown when she dropped lettuce on a sketch for Kelly's dress, it was impossible to believe he and Ben had been talking about the same person. The Willow Ben described sounded as mercenary about love as he was, as absorbed in appearance and what others thought, caring more about being seen in the right places and with the right people than helping others.

The Willow Eli was growing to know—care for, even—was a million miles away from that.

So which one of them was wrong?

Ben had known her intimately for years, so Eli had to assume it was him—he only had a couple of weeks of friendly encounters with her, after all. She could be putting on an act for him to get back at Ben.

Except…except Eli would bet his whole life savings that he knew her better than his brother did.

And that just made no sense at all.

'Do you need help getting all that home?' he asked, long after lunch, when she packed up to leave. It was an idiotic thing to say, a stupid offer, just asking for trouble. But he made it anyway because he couldn't resist spending just a little while longer in her company. To prove that he was right about her.

That she was honest and good and not the woman his brother talked about.

Willow hesitated, her arms full of fabric samples and who knew what else. How had she even got them all there? He hoped she'd taken a cab.

'Don't you have work you need to do here?' she asked. 'I know I've been taking up a lot of your time lately.' The way she chewed on her lower lip as she awaited his answer told him she knew they were playing with fire here too. But she hadn't asked him not to come.

Eli looked at the screen, full of unanswered emails he hadn't been able to focus on anyway. They'd keep until he was at home tonight, unable or unwilling to sleep. 'Nah.'

And so he found himself back in her cavernous apartment, drinking a beer she'd insisted he stay for, while she got on with the job at hand. He couldn't even bring himself to regret it, even if the whole situation was bound to blow up in his face sooner or later.

The sewing machine that dominated the oversized coffee table hadn't been there the last time he'd visited, he was sure. Neither had the stack of glossy magazines with designer dresses and gowns in them. Or the basket full of fabric samples and what he assumed were the things his maternal grandmother had always referred to as 'sewing notions'.

'Are you making Kelly's actual dress right now?' he asked, as she measured out a fabric on the floor that looked a lot plainer than the ones Kelly had been sighing over earlier.

Willow shook her head, not looking away from the task at hand. 'This is the mock-up for her to try on, to make sure it works right, before I start cutting the actual fabric she chose—that's a lot more expensive, so I want to make any mistakes on this stuff first.'

'That makes sense.' Sitting down on the sofa to watch her work, he realised that this small living area was the only part of the apartment that looked lived in at all. The rest was still bare and empty, while the area around the coffee table looked like a sewing shop had exploded in it. 'Wouldn't this be easier at the dining table?'

'Better light over here,' Willow answered. 'Besides, I'm scared of all that glass.'

'I can understand that.' But not why she chose to live here. An apartment less suited to the woman he was coming to know was hard to imagine.

Maybe Ben had helped her choose it.

Eli swallowed down the guilt that rose in his gullet at the thought, and focused on the woman in front of him. It was easy, watching her work, to forget that she was anything to do with his brother's supermodel girlfriend. She seemed a whole different person around him.

For a while, he just watched her as she drew around pattern pieces and measured cut fabric, her bottom lip trapped between her teeth as she concentrated. It was fascinating to him. He wondered if Ben had ever seen her like this.

And that was the thought that stunned him out of his silent reverie again.

'How did you learn to do all this?' he asked, just to stop himself staring obsessively. 'You said your sister taught you?'

'Uh...yeah.' Willow placed two pieces of fabric together and started to pin them. 'One summer when we were about, um, seventeen, I think, she got it into her head to learn to make her own clothes—rather than relying on the ones designers gave us. I'd...um, she'd been spending a lot of time with the stylists back stage at our shows, and she was always fascinated by the way they made clothes look perfect, even as we were halfway onto the runway—tacking up a hem, fixing a shoulder seam, anything that had been missed at the fitting or what have you. Anyway, she spent a whole summer in our London townhouse teaching herself from videos on the internet. And she got kind of good at it.'

'So you asked her to teach you too?'

'Exactly.' Willow looked away, her focus completely on the dress in front of her.

Eli was missing something here. He wasn't sure what it was, but there was definitely something. Something to do with her sister? Something she was afraid of telling him?

Afraid? That couldn't be right. Could it?

But he knew this feeling. The rising bubbles of frustration in his chest. The heavy weight of being left out in the cold, the only one who didn't know the truth.

He'd felt it his whole childhood, with the rumours about his parentage.

But he'd felt it as an adult too—when he'd realised the girl he thought he'd loved, or at least *could* love, was sleeping with his brother. Ben had denied it, of course, until the girl confessed all. Ben had apologised profusely—but in a way that had somehow left Eli feeling it was *his* fault for not realising the girl wasn't serious about him sooner.

He felt as if he was waiting for another one of those apologies.

Except this time *he* was the one in the wrong, wasn't he? He was the one lusting after his brother's girl—although at least they were actually broken up, this time. For now.

Maybe that was it. Maybe Willow just didn't want to tell him that she still loved his brother, that whatever he thought was happening between them, the connection he felt, it was all in his mind.

Yeah. That had to be it. What else *could* it be?

Eli drained the rest of his beer, put the bottle down on the table and got to his feet.

'I'll leave you to it, then,' he said.

Willow looked up sharply. 'Okay. Thanks for…well. I'll see you soon.'

He nodded. 'Soon.'

But only if he couldn't avoid it.

He needed to stay away from Willow Harper—at least until the charity gala.

Otherwise, he was afraid he might lose his mind.

The mock-up dress was finished.

Rowan studied it through narrowed eyes as it hung on the adjustable dress form she'd ordered on Willow's credit card. Obviously, it was nowhere near as grand as the finished dress would be, but already the lines hung well, and she could imagine it on Kelly's curvaceous body, looking fantastic.

She'd hoped to have it done sooner, but, well. It had been a couple of nights since Eli had left the apartment so abruptly. She hadn't been able to concentrate with him watching her, but she'd found she couldn't concentrate with him gone either. Not when she didn't know what thought process had made him leave.

Had he begun to suspect something? She'd almost slipped up when he'd asked about 'her sister' learning to make dresses—almost let slip that it was her, not Willow. And after that he'd been watching her so closely, asking questions about her 'sister'…and she'd wanted to tell him everything. To tell him about herself, her past, her life, with him knowing she was talking about *herself.*

She wanted to tell him she was Rowan, not Willow.

But how could she?

She'd made a promise to her sister. To her unborn niece or nephew. After everything

Willow had done for her, this was all she needed in return. Rowan couldn't screw it up.

No. The only thing to do was to try to carry on as if everything was normal. Not normal for Willow, as she'd never be in this position, and not normal for Rowan, because that was home in Rumbelow. Normal for Rowan *pretending* to be Willow.

It was giving her a headache, this feeling that she was two different people at the same time. She wasn't even sure which one was most real any more.

But normal, in this bizarre version of reality, was heading down to the Launch offices with this mock-up dress for Kelly to try on, so she could make any adjustments she needed to before she started cutting the fabric for the real thing.

She grabbed a coffee on her way, hoping it would give her a little more energy after three nights of little sleep, and also because it meant Eli couldn't offer her one at the office and she'd be able to make a quick getaway.

In fact, she lucked out—Eli wasn't even there when she arrived. The receptionist gave her a friendly smile before handing over the visitor lanyard Rowan had started to think of as her own, and waving her towards the lifts.

In the office, she found Kelly organising files on Eli's desk.

'Boss isn't in,' she said. 'I assumed he was slacking off with you.'

'Afraid not. But it doesn't matter.' Rowan held up the dress bag with the mock-up in it. 'I'm here to see you anyway.'

Kelly squealed and grabbed the bag, disappearing into the ladies' bathroom to put it on.

'Don't forget, it's just the mock-up!' Rowan called after her.

She perched on the edge of Eli's desk while she waited, casting a glance over the papers Kelly had been sorting. She wasn't snooping, she told herself. Just…surveying her surroundings.

Which happened to include a bright yellow sticky note, right on the top of the pile, with the words *Your brother—call back!* in stark black letters.

Ben had called Eli. *Call back.* Did that mean he wanted Eli to call him back, or that he was returning Eli's call? Rowan couldn't be sure.

And if Eli had been calling Ben…what if it was about her? What if he *knew*?

At that moment, Kelly emerged from the bathroom—beaming and strutting as if she were on a catwalk, not weaving between the desks of her office. Rowan clapped her hands in delight at how well the mock-up dress fell around her. Then she turned a more critical eye on her work, and busied herself making the tiny alterations that made all the difference in a bespoke dress.

She accompanied Kelly into the bathroom to help her out of the dress again, since it was now filled with pins and probably a dangerous solo task. By the time she came back out, Eli was sitting behind his desk, frowning at the sticky note on top of his files.

Rowan's heart did a quick double beat, and she silently told it to act normal. If Eli was starting to suspect something, the last thing she should do was panic. In fact, she needed to behave as if her life was perfectly ordinary.

Even when that was the furthest possible thing from the truth.

He looked up as she approached and smiled—but it wasn't the smile she was used to. It wasn't the open, friendly, welcoming smile she loved to see. It was tight and reserved and she didn't like it one bit.

He knows.

He can't know.

And he can't find out.

Already, she could feel the alarm rising, her chest tightening, and she forced herself to focus on her breathing. On the present moment, right now. Usually, she did that by noticing things around her.

Five things I can see. Four things I can hear.

Except this time all she could see, hear or think about was Eli.

'I thought you might be here,' he said, and her heart stuttered again. Then he nodded towards her bags, abandoned by the side of his desk. 'Those were a giveaway.'

'Right. Sorry.' She gathered them up over his protestations that it was fine. 'I had the mock-up ready for Kelly to try on. And now I'm going to go home and start sewing the real thing, so—'

Juggling her bags, the mock-up dress and her empty reusable coffee cup, she lost her balance, and everything tumbled to the ground— including her. Or she would have done, if it hadn't been for Eli's strong grip on her arm.

'Willow,' he said firmly. 'I wasn't asking you to leave.'

He was so close now she could see the fine lines around his concerned eyes. And apparently he could see the shadows under hers because he said, 'You look tired.'

She pulled away from his grip and began gathering her things again. 'Just what every girl wants to hear.'

She regretted the words as soon as she'd said them. Why should she care what Eli thought about her looks? She was supposed to be pining after his brother or something, wasn't she?

He flinched anyway. 'I just meant…is everything okay?'

Oh, he meant had she had any more anxiety attacks without him there to talk her down. 'Everything's fine.' Even if the only thing making her anxious right now was him.

Or the secrets she was keeping from him, more accurately.

'Okay. Good.' He looked at her for a long moment, his eyes moving as if he was searching for something in her own gaze. Then he sighed. 'Listen, there's a cocktails and canapés thing for gala sponsors tonight. I meant… I should have invited you earlier. I know it's short notice, but it would be great if you could come.'

Off to the side, Kelly was giving her boss a puzzled look Rowan couldn't quite understand, but it gave her pause all the same. 'I…'

She glanced down at the desk, at the sticky note about Ben, almost involuntarily.

'Ben won't be there,' Eli said quickly. 'If you're worried about bumping into him. That…that message is about something else.'

Something he wasn't telling her. Not that there was any real reason he should.

Rowan considered her options. Say no, offend Eli, let down the charity perhaps, and spend the evening alone, fretting over what he suspected.

Or go to the event, enjoy Eli's company—and maybe even figure out why Kelly was looking at him that way, and what was going on with his brother.

Put like that…

'I'd love to come,' she said.

Eli picked Willow up from her apartment that evening, braced for a night of trying not to touch her. Or even look at her, probably, if he didn't want to give his feelings away.

Kelly at the office already suspected, he knew. Hell, half the staff probably did, if they'd seen them together. But Kelly was particularly suspicious because he'd told her, when she was finalising the list for that night's event, that Willow couldn't make it.

And then he'd gone and asked her in front of Kelly, making it obvious that he'd never mentioned it to her in the first place.

Way to give himself away.

He hadn't intended to invite her at all. His plan of trying to keep his distance had been working well, at least until he saw her there in the office, looking tired but proud. He was proud of her too. Kelly's dress might not be finished yet, but he could already tell it would be stunning. More than that, just the time she'd given his assistant counted for so much. He was fond of Kelly, in a big brother sort of way, and it was so nice to see someone else realise how special she was.

So yes. He'd tried keeping his distance from Willow. But really, what was the point? She was in his life now. A sponsor at his gala event, and yes, maybe as his brother's girlfriend again once more. He couldn't change that. He wasn't even going to try.

Whatever else had passed between them over the years, Ben was his brother. He wouldn't betray him.

But Willow... He'd grown to care for her since the day she'd found him in her apartment. They had a connection. And perhaps it was foolish to try and ignore that too.

So he'd invited her tonight. And if part of his reason was that, knowing Ben was back in the country, it was only a matter of time before their easy friendship would have to come to an end, he intended to ignore that. At least for tonight.

Thankfully, she wasn't wearing that fire-engine-red dress again. Tonight's outfit was, instead, a shimmering golden dress that fell halfway down her calf. The thin spaghetti straps admittedly looked like they could give way at any moment, and Eli knew he'd be dreaming that night about peeling them from her shoulders. She had paired the dress with matching high heels, her hair piled up in some sort of complicated fashion on top of her head. She looked every inch the su-permodel—and completely out of his reach.

He had to remember that.

No touching.

If he touched her, he might lose his mind.

'So what is tonight about?' Willow asked as she settled into the front passenger seat of his car.

'It was Kelly's idea, actually,' Eli replied. 'She had the thought that, if all of these rich people were supporting the same charity, they might have more in common than they thought. So if we brought them together before the main event, it would give them a chance to mingle and network.'

'Potentially giving them new business contacts as well,' Willow said. 'Clever. You've given them more than they expected—more than just a chance to do good. You've given them a business opportunity too.'

'That's the hope,' Eli said as he pulled away from the kerb. 'We need these people to do more than donate just once a year for this gala night, even if it is our biggest fundraising opportunity on the calendar. We need regular ongoing support to keep our work going. If our sponsors feel they can get more value from us by being part of what we're trying to do all year round, that can only help us out.'

The venue for the night's event was a hotel uptown that Eli had never made it to before, but was supposed to be the next big thing. Willow, he was sure, must have been there a hundred times before, but she still managed to look impressed as they walked into the flashy lobby, and through to the bar area Kelly had hired for the evening.

Already, the room was bustling, and as they walked through to the bar Eli heard numerous conversations between unlikely companions about everything from golf to family to business. One or two of them were even talking about the work Launch was doing there in the city, which was gratifying.

It didn't take long for Eli to get drawn into conversation with a backer or two. To start with, Willow stayed by his side—but then Sandra appeared and the next time he checked, the two women were off together by the bar.

It *was* a work event, so Eli tried not to be frustrated that so many supporters wanted his time and attention. Normally, he'd be in his element—he loved talking about Launch, the work they did, the kids they'd helped and where they were now—at college, or undertaking apprenticeships, or setting up their own businesses, or starting families that had the right tools to be better adjusted than the ones they came from.

But tonight he just wanted to be with Willow. To enjoy what was left of his time with her.

Ben was out of town again this weekend and, from the way he'd gone back to dodging his calls—the message on the sticky note on his desk had proved to be a call from Ben's assistant saying that Ben didn't have time to speak to him this week—he might even have a suspicion of what was up. He and Willow hadn't been discreet in their adventures around town, and people always did love to talk. Plus, he knew there was always a chance of a photographer being about when Willow left her apartment. Just because they hadn't seen the camera flash, or spotted any resulting photo on the internet, didn't mean it wasn't there—or that Ben hadn't seen it. Hell, if he suspected something, he might even have hired a PI to tail her.

So this could be his last night with Willow. And he was spending it talking to other people.

No wonder he was frustrated.

He had to make do with glimpses of that shimmering dress across the room, as Sandra introduced her to anyone and everyone she might like to meet. Or, knowing Sandra, donors who would be excited and grateful to meet Willow—and maybe give a little more next time. She wasn't his best fundraiser by chance.

But as the event started to wind down, and he was just allowing himself to think about asking Willow to join him at the jazz bar around the corner that he liked, he realised that Sandra was by the door saying goodbye to people—and Willow was nowhere to be seen.

'If you'll excuse me.' He extricated himself from his current conversation with an apologetic smile, and set out to find her.

It took only a moment to establish that she wasn't in the main bar—the crowd had thinned out enough that he could see it all in a glance. Perhaps she'd gone to the ladies' bathrooms? He should have thought of that sooner. Willow was hardly likely to thank him for storming in there in a panic looking for her.

But he was *responsible* for her. He'd brought her here. And the funny, unsettled feeling behind his ribs told him that something wasn't right here.

When Sandra confessed she hadn't seen her for a while that feeling solidified, and Eli decided he didn't care how mad she was with him for overreacting, he was going to find her. Now.

After just a few words with the concierge, he had a team helping search inside. Which left him the outside. It was possible she'd wanted to get some air; the room had been stifling at its most crowded. And overwhelming, perhaps.

The thought of Willow suffering another panic attack without him set him into even faster action. Eschewing the elevator, he took the stairs three at a time to the fourth floor, and then up one more to the roof terrace. He burst out into the high-level garden, and spotted a tell-tale shimmer of golden light almost instantly. Not wanting to alarm her, he put a hand out to stop the doors slamming shut. And then he watched, and listened.

'No, really, I need to get back inside now,' Willow was saying, firmly but politely. 'Thank you for showing me the sights—you're right, the view is spectacular. But my date will be waiting.'

Date. She had to mean him, even if it wasn't strictly an accurate term. But the fact she felt she needed to use it...

Willow made to move towards the doors, where he stood hidden in the shadows, still unseen. But the man at her side reached out to grab her around the waist, pulling her close. She pushed him away, but he only held her tighter.

Eli blinked away the red mist that threatened to fill his vision. Willow didn't need him to come in fists flying. She needed an accomplice to get her out of there without a scene.

He pulled the roof terrace door open again and, this time, let it slam closed. 'Willow? Are you up here? I just asked the guy to bring the car around. Shall we get going?'

The man beside her let go at the sound of his voice, just as he'd hoped. Eli didn't recognise him as anyone *he'd* spoken to that night, but he made a point of memorising his face so he could quiz Sandra later about who he might be.

Willow hurried to his side. 'Of course,' she said brightly. 'I was just taking a look at the view. But I'm done now.'

Eli held the door open for her and, this time, headed for the elevator. They waited in nervous silence for the car to arrive, but the man didn't follow.

'Who was he?' Eli asked, once the elevator doors had closed behind them, and he'd punched the button for the ground floor.

Willow shook her head. 'I don't know. Someone from the party. I was trying to politely excuse myself by saying I wanted to get some air, and then he insisted on taking me up to the roof garden and, well. You saw the rest, I imagine.'

Eli shook his head. 'If I hadn't come up when I did...'

'Then I would have kneed him in the groin and come down alone,' Willow said firmly. 'And if that didn't work, I had pepper spray *and* a rape alarm in my bag. I didn't need you to save me, Eli.'

'No. I know.' That didn't change the fact that he was glad he *had* been there. Just in case.

They travelled down in silence for another second or two before Willow slipped her hand through his arm, and he realised she was shaking a little. 'I'm really glad you did, though.'

He covered her hand with his own. 'Me too.'

CHAPTER SEVEN

'WELL? HOW DO I look?' Kelly stepped out of the women's bathrooms at the Launch offices to a full-on round of applause, and more than a few whistles—mostly from the women.

The dress Rowan had spent the last week sewing looked *exactly* like she'd imagined it in her head, more so even than it had on paper, and she beamed at Kelly as the relief flooded through her.

She'd done it. Even while pretending to be her sister, she'd created a dress that made someone smile. Made them feel like Cinderella going to the ball.

Maybe it wasn't as noble a calling as Eli's, but it was hers, and she was proud of it.

'You've done an amazing job,' Eli murmured next to her ear as he leaned against his desk beside her. 'I've never seen Kelly smile so much. Thank you.'

'It was a pleasure,' Rowan said honestly,

ignoring the slight shiver that found its way down her spine at the feel of his voice by her skin.

She couldn't help but imagine those lips *on* her skin. Even though she knew she mustn't.

Ever since the night on the roof terrace, the week before, the pull between them had seemed stronger than ever.

Rowan hadn't been lying; she could have handled herself with that man. She'd been in worse situations before and managed alone. And she knew his type; he was all talk, but he wouldn't have taken it any further. Especially not in such a public place.

She wasn't blasé about the risks a woman faced alone in the city, though. She hadn't been lying about the pepper spray or the rape alarm either. In fact, she'd had the first of them tight in her grip inside her bag when she'd heard Eli's voice.

It was funny, she supposed, that an event like that hadn't sparked an anxiety attack, whereas the thought of Eli finding out her secret made her breathing catch instantly. Perhaps because she'd known she was in control, had known her next steps and what she would do to save herself.

If Eli found out the truth… Rowan had no idea what she would do next, then.

But if he went on believing she was Willow, that she was in love with his brother, until she left New York…if he never knew the truth at all…she wasn't sure what she'd do then either.

This hadn't been the plan. She was never supposed to meet Eli, let alone grow so close to him.

She wasn't supposed to be lying to anyone she cared about. Just a few photographers or designers who cared more about what she looked like than who she was, anyway.

Eli cared who she was.

But she wasn't who she said she was.

That was a problem neither she nor Willow had seen coming.

She'd lain awake for nights, wondering what would happen when the real Willow returned. Would she just avoid Eli for ever? Feign amnesia of the whole affair?

In the end there had only been one answer.

Once the gala was over, Rowan needed to walk away. To prove to everyone that all of this had only been about helping the children who needed Launch to make their lives better. After that…what reason would she have to see Eli again, anyway?

So she'd walk away. And then, when Willow came back to New York, she'd have no reason to see him. Especially if she really didn't plan to get back together with Ben.

If she handled this right, she and Willow could keep all their secrets. And Eli might wonder, might even feel let down, but that was all.

And it was something Rowan would have to live with.

'Willow? Can you help me out of this thing?' Kelly asked as she turned back towards the bathrooms. 'I don't want to risk getting *anything* on my perfect princess dress before my big night!'

'Of course.' Rowan pushed away from the desk and forced herself not to glance back at Eli as she followed Kelly. She felt his gaze on her all the same.

Kelly was bubbling with excitement about the gala and her dress as Rowan helped her change back into her office-wear, storing the dress carefully in the protective bag she'd delivered it in.

'What are *you* wearing, though?' Kelly asked, as she fluffed her hair in the mirror.

'I haven't really thought about it yet,' Rowan admitted. She'd have to, though, and soon. Willow would have something suitable in her wardrobe, she was sure.

Kelly gave her a sideways look. 'You do realise that that gala is *tomorrow,* right?'

'I know, I know. I just…well, I've been more worried about your dress than mine!'

'Girl, I know you look incredible in anything, and you must have a closet *full* of gowns. But don't you want to wear something that really knocks the boss's socks off tomorrow night?'

Rowan froze, aware that in the mirror her reflection looked paler than ever. 'Um… Eli and I…it's really not like that. I mean, I'm his brother's ex-girlfriend.'

'*Ex* being the important word in that sentence.' Kelly turned to rest a hip against the sink and gave her a serious look. 'Willow. If any man looked at me the way Eli looks at you? I'd have him down the aisle faster than he could blink.'

'I don't—'

Kelly held up a hand. 'And the way you look at him? That's no better either. You want him, and he wants you, that much is obvious to anyone with eyes. But more than that…

You two are good for each other. I've never seen Eli as happy—in himself as much as in work—as he has been these last few weeks. And as for you...' She shook her head. 'I don't know much about that brother of his—and I want to know even less—but from what I've seen and heard and read...he's not the right guy for you. Is he. Honestly?'

Rowan shook her head. That much, at least, was easy to agree on.

'So why let the past—or him—ruin what could be a really great relationship for you and Eli?' Kelly asked.

'It's not that simple.' Because it wasn't the past, or Ben, keeping them apart. It was the lies she'd been telling since the day they'd met. And if she walked away he'd believe those lies for the rest of his life.

But it was the only answer. Unless...

I tell him the truth, she realised suddenly, and a weight landed on her chest at the same time as another one lifted from her shoulders.

Because the truth might only make things worse.

'Just think about it,' Kelly advised as she took her dress from Rowan and opened the bathroom door.

'I will,' Rowan promised.

An easy promise, since she already knew that question wasn't going to let her sleep tonight.

Eli had intended to pick Willow up for the gala dinner, like he had on every other night they'd gone out together. But by mid-afternoon on the day of the event it was already clear that wasn't going to be a possibility.

'I'll meet you there,' he told Willow, his phone jammed between his ear and his shoulder as he scanned the pile of forms Kelly had just thrust into his hands. 'Will you be all right getting there on your own?'

'I think I can just about manage,' Willow said dryly.

And now the night they'd been working towards all year was finally here. But rather than enjoying the moment, Eli found all he could do was scan the crowds looking for one particular woman.

The venue they'd chosen was stunning. Somehow, Kelly had managed to find a botanical garden he'd never heard of that was looking to get into the wedding venue business, and given them an incredible deal to come in and try it all out.

It had been a risk, Eli knew, but the more

money they could save on running the event, the more the final total raised. And so far it seemed to be paying off.

'I can't believe you found this place,' he told a beaming Kelly as, together, they surveyed their surroundings. Lights had been strung everywhere, hidden amongst the foliage and wound around wooden pagodas and structures that lined the paths. A band played in one corner of the gardens and people were even dancing to the big band music that filled the air. One of the smaller vintage-looking glasshouses had been transformed into a bar, with a silent auction ongoing inside, hoping to draw a few more big donations.

Later, they'd wind their way down one of the starlit paths to the larger glasshouse, where dinner would be served. Eli had already seen it, with its crisp white linen on the tables, the lights hanging from retro wires from the roof, and the greenery wound all through it until it was impossible to tell where the garden ended and the dining room began.

While most of the guests were donors— and people they wanted to impress—there were also staff, thanks to Willow, sitting at the Launch table. Also present were some of their success stories, as Sandra put it. Kids they'd helped out of terrible situations and, with the kids own hard work, supported them onto better paths. Eli knew Sandra had briefed them all, asking them to talk up the work they did, to show how well it worked.

'*Social proof,*' she'd told him seriously. '*Anecdotes from those kids will work better than any statistics we throw at them.*'

But Kelly had also made a suggestion that Eli had embraced, and they'd invited a number of the kids they were helping right now too. Ones who *weren't* success stories yet—but could be.

And right now, Eli could see those kids mingling with some of the biggest names in NYC business, eyes wide, helping themselves to canapés. If nothing else, they'd have shown them the sort of life that was possible—something they might never have known, otherwise.

'Seriously, Kelly,' he said. 'This place is incredible.'

She smiled smugly. 'New York Botanical Garden? Brooklyn Botanical Garden? Those are for suckers.'

'And out of our price range for the events budget,' Eli added, which was rather more the reason they hadn't picked either of the more famous gardens.

'And that,' Kelly allowed. 'But the point remains; this is the place to be. And I am dressed to party!'

'You are that.' The dress Willow had made fit Kelly like a dream, and enhanced and celebrated her personality, her body, and her confidence. He'd never seen his assistant look quite so alive. 'You should go enjoy it.'

'You sure?' Kelly gave him a worried look. 'I can wait with you until Willow gets here? Or just drag you over to talk to all the people you're *supposed* to be schmoozing, if you weren't too busy mooning over a certain model we both know.'

'I'm not mooning.'

'Boss.' Kelly laid a hand on his arm and looked up at him, her eyes serious. 'You really, really are.' Then her gaze flicked away to something happening to his right. 'So why don't you go do something about that?'

Kelly melted away into the crowd as he turned around, and there was Willow, the people parting to let her through as if the whole botanical garden was her catwalk.

He tried not to let his mouth fall open at the sight of her, but he honestly wasn't sure if he'd succeeded or not. If he'd been blown away by the dresses she'd worn on previous nights, nothing had prepared him for tonight's gown.

It was black and white, fell all the way to the floor and—crucially—was strapless. In fact, Eli assumed the thing was only staying up from sheer force of will. Or perhaps because it fitted so closely to her torso, before flaring out into a wide skirt with a slit that ran…oh, God. It ran all the way up to her mid-thigh.

She looked stunning—a point that was lost on none of the people she walked past.

She looked…she looked like she always did in the photos in magazines. The ones where she was on Ben's arm, going to some flashy event or another.

That thought brought him back down to earth, fast. And when she reached him, he struggled to return her smile.

'Everything okay?' she asked, looking concerned.

'Everything's fine.'

Except I've fallen for my brother's ex, who he probably expects to get back together with any moment. And she's so far out of my reach I shouldn't even be able to see her.

But he could. And that fact was doing things to him.

'Is it the dress?' Willow looked down at herself, dismayed. 'I was worried it was too much. But when I sent Kelly a photo, she said it was perfect.'

'It is perfect.' His voice sounded gravelly, even to his own ears. 'You look perfect.'

Perfect for Ben. Not for him.

'Okay. Good.' Willow was still eyeing him sideways, like she was trying to figure out what was wrong with him.

But it wasn't like he could tell her, was it?

Kelly came to his rescue, thankfully, although she shot him an accusatory look as she did it. 'Willow, you're here!'

The two women appreciated each other's dresses, and then Kelly whisked her off to chat to some of the kids she'd met at the Castaway Café the other week. But not before she paused to whisper at him, 'That was lame, boss. Very, very lame.'

And the worst part was, Eli knew she was right.

Rowan had decided, even before leaving the apartment, that she was going to channel Willow for the evening.

Everyone at this event would be expecting Willow Harper, supermodel and socialite—not her anxious, awkward and uncomfortable minutes-younger sister who hadn't sashayed down a catwalk in years.

So she'd picked the most Willow-like gown she could find in the wardrobe, and even helped herself to her sister's lipstick and perfume. And she'd given herself a stern talking-to in the mirror while waiting for her cab too.

'You are Willow tonight. And Willow would walk in there with her head high and her back straight. She wouldn't notice all the people staring at her. She'd smile and be gracious and charming, and make friends with all the important people who matter. So that's what you'll do too.' Then she'd nodded at her reflection, grabbed her clutch bag and headed down to the lobby to wait for her cab, hoping she'd get used to the high heels before she arrived.

To start with, things had gone exactly to plan. People had stared as she'd stepped out of the cab, but while she'd felt their gazes on her, she'd focused on her own body—on her senses, and her breathing—to help her ignore them.

She'd mastered the heels—grateful for the

solid path through the gardens that meant she didn't sink into the grass. She'd even managed a small sashay as she walked.

But then she'd reached Eli. And while she'd hoped that his stunned expression might just be her breathtaking beauty, she hadn't really been all that optimistic. Because all along, what she looked like was the thing Eli had cared about least.

There was something wrong there, and she couldn't ask what it was—not here, not tonight. Maybe he'd already figured out the truth, or maybe there was something else going on with Ben he didn't want to tell her about. But she couldn't ask him tonight.

She needed to tell him the truth about who she was, if he *hadn't* figured it out. She'd already decided that. Walking away just wasn't an option any more, which meant confessing was the only way through.

And while part of her wanted to do that right now and get it over with...

Not tonight.

Eli and his team had been working for *months* on tonight's gala event, and she was damned if she was going to make it all about her, when he should be enjoying the spotlight and doing the good work that mattered so much to him.

So she didn't press, after her initial polite query. She let Kelly lead her away gratefully— and pretended she didn't hear her whispered comment to her boss.

With a glass of champagne in her hand she was happy to do the rounds with Kelly—but even happier when she got to talk to some of the kids she'd met at the Castaway Café, rather than the titans of industry she'd been preparing for. Their overawed excitement about the event echoed her own; they'd certainly never had anything like this in Rumbelow, although she wasn't sure she wouldn't rather be at folk night at the local pub.

Before she'd left home, and modelling, behind for good, she'd always tried to avoid the big events. At least this one was outdoors, which meant she got plenty of fresh air. The worst were the ones where she could feel the walls closing in, as the voices around her grew louder and louder, matched only by the thumping of blood in her ears.

She didn't see Eli again until they were led through for dinner. She looked for him as the staff—dressed in white dinner jackets— started to usher them down a path through a tree tunnel towards the dining area, but she couldn't spot him. She assumed he must have gone on ahead to get things sorted, and took the arm of a kindly-looking older gentleman in a tailcoat to lead her through.

The glasshouse where the dinner was being served was spectacular; Rowan gasped when she saw it, and from the noise around her, she wasn't the only one.

'It's like a magical garden,' she whispered. 'I half expect a talking bird to flutter past at any moment.'

The man beside her chuckled. 'I wouldn't put it past that brother-in-law of yours. He'll do anything to help his cause—an admirable trait, I suppose, but it does strain the wallet rather!'

He wandered off to find his table, leaving Rowan to wrap her arms around herself at his words. *Brother-in-law.*

He wasn't, of course, not even Willow's. But the guy clearly wasn't up on the celebrity gossip and thought Ben and Willow were still together. Maybe most people in the room did.

She'd have to remember that. She didn't want to trash her sister's reputation by being seen mooning over her supposed boyfriend's brother—especially if, in the end, Willow went back to Ben to raise their child together.

There was a beautiful seating plan, edged in vines and flowers, that guided her to the table she'd sponsored—on Willow's credit card. She was pleased to see that she recognised most of the people sitting there—either from the office, or from the Castaway Café. With Kelly on her right, keeping the conversation flowing, she was able to relax a bit and enjoy the meal.

But not completely. At the edge of her awareness, she couldn't ignore the pull to look at Eli, sitting up with the big donors at the front table. He seemed perfectly relaxed, enjoying his evening, and oblivious to her sitting across the room.

Good. That was good.

'I'm sure he wishes you were sitting up there with him too,' Kelly murmured in her ear, thankfully quiet enough that no one else at the table seemed to hear.

'I don't know what you're talking about,' Rowan lied, and made a point of not looking over at Eli's table for the rest of the meal.

It wasn't until after dessert had been served and eaten, and Kelly and several of her other tablemates had disappeared to the bathrooms, when she felt that awareness again. Someone was watching her—she could feel all the hairs on the back of her neck standing up. *Eli*.

She turned towards his table, but he was deep in conversation with the woman next to him, and not looking her way at all. So who—?

'Willow!' A tall, handsome man about her own age tumbled into Kelly's chair, and reached out to pull her into a hug. 'It's so good to see you again! Where's Ben?' He looked around him rather obviously at the lack of Eli's brother. 'You two aren't on the outs again, are you?'

Rowan smiled tightly, desperately scanning her memory for any picture of this guy from Willow's press photos, but coming up with nothing. She had no idea who he was, but he clearly knew her—or, rather, Willow— very well.

'He couldn't make it tonight,' she said shortly. That was simple enough, right? It was reasonable to assume that if he *could* have made the most important date in his brother's year he would have done.

But the man gave a short, nasty laugh. 'I bet he couldn't. So, he sent you to represent, did he? Good of you to still do it, given those photos that came out earlier.'

'Photos?' Rowan blurted, before she could stop herself. Of what? They couldn't be of Willow in Rumbelow, could they?

'Oh, don't say you haven't seen them? I've really put my foot in it now, haven't I?' He pulled a face that was probably supposed to be remorseful, but somehow just looked smug.

Rowan pushed her chair away from her table. 'I'm sorry. I just need to—' She didn't elaborate, stumbling blindly through the tables towards the exit, just hoping she didn't break an ankle in Willow's heels.

She'd been an idiot to think she could do this. Of course she was going to bump into Willow's so-called friends, and she had no idea who any of them were, or what their agendas were—because they clearly had them. And what the hell had Ben been photographed doing, anyway?

Outside the glasshouse, she leaned against the cool bark of the nearest tree and pulled her phone from her clutch bag to do an internet search. It only took seconds to find the photos of Ben cavorting on the deck of some yacht somewhere with a curvaceous brunette in a tiny bikini.

Rowan rolled her eyes. Fine. As long as Willow was still safe and enjoying some privacy back home in England, she didn't much care what her sister's ex was up to.

'Willow?' Eli appeared from the glasshouse, his bow tie skewwhiff and his eyes concerned. 'Are you okay? I saw Jack corner you, dripping his usual poison, I assume. What was it this time?'

Rowan turned her phone towards Eli with a wry smile. 'He just wanted to make sure I'd seen these.'

Eli studied the photos for a second and went very still, his mouth little more than a line above his tightened jaw. Then he said, 'My brother is an utter, utter idiot, Willow, and he never deserved you.'

'We're broken up,' Rowan said evenly. The last thing she wanted to do was start some sort of feud between the brothers at this point.

'Again,' Eli replied. 'And he'll expect you to come back to him again when he wants you, and ignore anything he did when you were apart, right?'

'Probably,' Rowan admitted, even though it wasn't exactly *her* Ben would be expecting. And she wasn't sure that Willow would go this time either, given the baby.

Eli met her gaze with his own burning one, and she realised there was more to this conversation than she'd expected. 'And that doesn't bother you? Because, Willow…if you were mine, the idea of anyone else touching you, even if we weren't together at that moment, I have to tell you, it would drive me insane.'

The heat in his words, the sincerity in his eyes, filled her with an emotion she'd forgotten, it had been so long since she'd felt it.

And when he leaned in closer, so near she could feel the heat of his breath against her mouth, she wanted nothing more than to kiss him. To feel his arms around her and his mouth on hers and his body—

Rowan pushed him away. 'Eli, no.'

CHAPTER EIGHT

ELI STUMBLED BACK so fast he almost fell over the vine growing up the tree behind him, or maybe his own feet, he wasn't really sure.

All he could hear was her 'no' echoing around the caverns of his mind.

He'd been wrong. Everything he'd thought was between them—the connection, the attraction…everything—had only been inside his head. He'd imagined it all.

It was almost enough to make him doubt his own sanity. Or, at the least, everything he thought he knew.

He'd been so *sure* she felt the way he did.

'Willow, I'm sorry.' The words tumbled out of him. 'I misread the situation. It's entirely on me, and I can't apologise enough for putting you in that position. I—'

But Willow was shaking her head. 'You didn't misread anything.'

Eli froze, staring back her. Her eyes were

wide, her pupils blown, and standing there in the glow of the tiny fairy lights wound around the branch above her head, she was the most beautiful thing he'd ever seen in his life.

'Then…is this about Ben? You're still in love with him?' Even after everything he'd done and said, if Willow really loved him and thought they could make things work, Eli couldn't get in the way of their possible happiness. He couldn't do that to his brother.

But Willow blew that idea out of the water too. 'It's not about Ben. I don't… I don't love him. *I* never did.'

The strange stress she put on the word *I* only confused him more. He shook his head to try to clear it, but it didn't help.

He made sure to keep back, not to crowd her, to give her the space to speak and think without him looming over her. Even if all he really wanted to do was pull her into his arms.

Whatever she said next…he hadn't imagined things between them. And she hadn't lied to him and told him that he had. That had to count for something.

Eli had been lied to enough in his life. Told that something he believed was wrong, when it was right. He didn't think he could take it if Willow did that to him too.

But she hadn't. She'd admitted the chemistry between them was mutual. And if the problem wasn't Ben...

'I don't understand, Willow. Can you explain it to me?'

She met his gaze, her expression open and vulnerable. 'I want to. But I... I'm scared how you're going to react.'

That hit him like a blow. 'You know I'd never hurt you, Willow, surely?'

'Of course.' That got him a small, tight smile. 'You just might not like me very much any more.'

'I honestly don't think that's possible,' he admitted. 'And I don't see how we can move forward from this moment if you *don't* tell me.'

'I know. And I... I'd already resolved to tell you the truth, anyway. I just didn't want to do it *tonight*. Tonight should be about you and your team, and all the hard work you've put in. Not about me and my sister and all our issues.'

'Your sister?' Eli frowned. 'The one who taught you to make dresses? What does she have to do with us?'

And then he knew. Before she even said the words, before her eyes dropped to the ground before she spoke so she wouldn't have to look him in the face. Before *everything* changed. He felt it, the truth of it, in his bones.

She wasn't Willow.

She took a breath. 'My sister didn't teach me how to make dresses. I taught her. Because I'm not Willow. I'm—'

'Rowan. You're Rowan.'

She nodded in confirmation, and Eli's whole world fractured.

He'd fallen for a woman who didn't exist. Who had lied to him about everything—even something as basic as her name.

He'd tortured himself with guilt over wanting his brother's ex. He'd told himself nothing could happen, that he was crazy for even thinking it.

But worst of all…he'd known there was something. Known she was keeping something from him, and he hadn't called her on it because he'd wanted so badly to believe her. To trust her.

And she'd blown that trust to smithereens.

'I'm sorry. I didn't want to lie. Hell, I didn't want to do this at all! Willow just showed up on my doorstep and—'

He held up a hand to stop her. He couldn't take any of this right now. Inside the glass-house, servers were clearing away the desserts and bringing out coffees. Any moment, someone was going to introduce him on that stage and he needed to be there to make a speech. To thank everyone for their donations, their support, their time—and encourage them to give more of all three.

He'd been writing and revising it for weeks. Now he couldn't remember the first line.

'Eli...' Willow started again.

No, not Willow, Rowan.

He shook his head anyway. 'I... I have to go give a speech.'

She stepped back, apology heavy in her eyes. 'I know. We can...can we talk about this later?'

He knew what she wanted to hear—that they could talk this out. That he'd listen to her explanation and try to understand what she'd done. That they'd work through their feelings together and build something stronger now they finally had a foundation of truth.

But he couldn't give her assurances on any of that right now. Not when he didn't think he could even *look* at her again.

So he just turned around and walked away,

back into the glasshouse, towards his real life, and all the people who were counting on him.

They were the ones that mattered right now.

And *they* hadn't lied to him.

Rowan watched Eli give his speech, her stomach churning and her head aching with all the could-have-beens and regrets spinning in it. Watching him, she was sure none of the other guests in the room could tell that she'd just ripped his heart out and stamped on it. That he'd just been betrayed in a horrible, horrible way.

She saw it now, more clearly than she had from inside her own deception.

She'd been thinking of Willow, of protecting her sister, protecting herself too if it came to it, and protecting her niece or nephew most of all. She'd thought that nobody needed to know. That no one would care.

But she'd been so very wrong.

From the other side of the lie, everything looked different.

She'd allowed herself to grow close to Eli—and for him to grow close to her—without being honest about something as basic as her name, her identity. She'd allowed him to believe that she was his brother's girl, so to speak. To feel guilty about everything that was brewing between them.

At the most basic level, she'd lied. When he'd felt there was something wrong, she'd brushed him off. She'd told him everything was fine, that she was Willow, that the world was flat and the sky was green—and he'd believed her. Because he'd trusted her.

But she wasn't worthy of that trust.

The audience laughed at one of the jokes in Eli's speech, and Rowan glanced up again to find his gaze on her. He put down the papers he was speaking from and stepped forward, right to the edge of the small platform they'd erected for the speeches.

'The kids we help…they get told a lot of lies in their lives,' he said, the tone of the room suddenly far more serious than it had been so far. 'From their parents, from their teachers, from their friends, from the world around them. On the one hand, you have a society that tells them they're nothing, worthless, and will probably end up dead or in prison. And on the other you have an American dream that tells them if they work hard they can be rich and happy and respected.

Which one is lying? Well, that, we've found, tends to be up to them.'

Eli wasn't looking directly at her any more, but she still knew, somehow, that his words were for her.

'When we lie to these kids and tell them they're worthless, that they can't make anything of themselves, we betray them, because sometimes all they need is a little faith to do incredible things. And at the same time, if we tell them that success and happiness is just a matter of hard work, that's a lie too— that path to the American dream looks a lot different depending on the circumstances you're born into, after all, and why should these kids judge themselves against someone with a trust fund and a family company to be given shares in—someone like me.'

That got a laugh, as Eli gave a self-deprecating shrug.

'The one thing we always promise the kids who come through our doors at the Castaway Café, or who make contact with Launch for help, is that we will never lie to them. Not about the ways we can help them, or—and this is the most important one—about *who they are. They* are the only ones who get to define that. We just want to help them—and we hope all of you will too. Thank you.'

He stepped down to overwhelming applause. Rowan joined in, but her mind was still whirling.

Was that what *she'd* done? Told Eli who he was by not telling him the truth about who she was? She supposed she had, in a way. He'd been defining himself in relation to her and their growing closeness, based on the idea that she was Willow.

And she really, really wasn't.

'Go talk to him,' Kelly said from beside her. When Rowan looked up, she rolled her eyes and continued. 'Whatever happened outside between you two, it's got you sighing and him ad-libbing the most important speech of his year—not that he didn't do a great job, of course. But go make it up before he does something else stupid that doesn't work out as well.'

'I'm not sure he wants to speak to me,' Rowan admitted.

'And that means you're not going to even try?' Kelly asked, brows raised.

No. No, it didn't.

But Rowan couldn't get close to him for the rest of the night. He was surrounded by donors, by friends, by the people this night was *supposed* to be about. So, in the end, she crept off to the taxi rank and headed home to Willow's apartment to make a call.

She needed to talk to her sister.

She needed to sort all this out.

Willow wasn't particularly pleased to be woken in what had to be the very early morning over in Rumbelow, but through her yawns she listened to what Rowan had to say all the same.

'Wait a minute,' she said, once Rowan was done. 'Are you sleeping with Ben's brother?'

'No! We're just friends,' Rowan insisted. 'I couldn't do anything more when I was still lying to him about something as basic as my actual name.'

'But you wanted to, right?' Willow guessed. 'That's why you felt you had to tell him the truth. I can get that.' She sighed heavily, and Rowan was pretty sure this was something more than tiredness.

'Is everything okay? With the baby? The cottage?' she asked. 'Ben hasn't been in touch, has he? Because, honestly, the more I hear about that guy, the more I think you had the right idea, hiding out in Rumbelow.'

'Even if it meant you had to make "friends" under false pretences?'

'Even then,' Rowan promised. 'Seriously, Will. Is everything okay?'

'Everything's fine,' Willow replied unconvincingly. 'There's just…stuff. But I had my next scan and we got to hear the baby's heartbeat and see it wriggling about and everything! Not enough for us to tell if it's a boy or a girl though. It had its legs crossed.'

'I want photos!' Rowan paused, and frowned. 'Wait. We?'

'Me and the ultrasound technician.'

Rowan was almost certain she was lying. But who else could possibly have been there with her? Nobody even knew she was in England.

'Right,' she said anyway. She had enough to worry about in New York without fretting about what was happening in Rumbelow too. Willow would tell her if she needed to worry. 'Well, send me photos.'

'I will,' Willow promised. 'If *you* talk to Eli. Tell him whatever you need to, just make sure he doesn't tell Ben where I am or what's going on.'

Tell him whatever you need to.

No. She couldn't do that.

There was only one thing she *could* tell Eli. 'I'm going to tell him the truth, Will.'

Eli hadn't wanted to come. Even now, standing outside Willow's apartment—or Rowan's, he wasn't really sure on any of that any more—he half wanted to turn around and walk away. More than half, if he was honest.

But Rowan had sounded so open and honest on the phone. She'd called and called until Kelly got sick of him refusing to take the calls, and told him it was a sponsor on the phone with an urgent problem who would only speak to him.

Which was, as she pointed out afterwards when he complained, strictly speaking, completely accurate.

So he'd spoken to Rowan—under false pretences—and she'd asked him to come. More than that, she'd promised to tell him *everything*. No lies, no confusion. Everything.

He wouldn't have come for anything less.

The door to the building opened without him buzzing or putting in a code, and suddenly Rowan was standing there in the open doorway.

'Are you coming up?' she asked, her head tipped slightly to the side as she watched him.

'Only this isn't really a conversation I can have in the street. That's why I asked you to come here.'

Oh, Eli had a very bad feeling about this. He had no idea what could make Rowan pretend to be her sister for weeks on end, but it wasn't going to be anything good, he was sure of that much.

His head had been whirling with possibilities ever since he'd realised the truth. He barely remembered anything of the gala after that moment with Rowan—not even the speech he gave which, apparently, went down thunderously well. Maybe someone had recorded it.

He'd barely slept afterwards, thinking of all the reasons Rowan might have had to lie to him.

He needed to know what the truth was.

'I'm coming up,' he said.

She didn't even look like Willow any more—which Eli knew was a ridiculous thing to say, since they were identical twins. And they *were* identical—in their physical looks, at least. But now he knew what he was looking for, Eli saw differences.

Whenever she'd been at the office or events as Willow, she'd carried herself a certain way—with a bearing that said she knew she belonged. She'd held her head high, and always seemed on a slightly different level— and not just because of her height in heels.

He'd seen glimpses behind that façade, though. The first time they'd met, at the apartment, when he'd helped her through an anxiety attack. And again at the Castaway Café, or when she was working on Kelly's dress.

Maybe those moments were the real Rowan.

And, if so, he knew he'd never forgive himself if he didn't at least give her the chance to explain.

So he watched her as she moved around the apartment kitchen, fixing drinks for them both. Her long blonde hair was caught up in a simple ponytail, and she wore plain slim-fitting jeans and a white T-shirt with a picture of a pineapple on it. Her feet were bare, the nails unpainted, and she had no make-up on her face, no jewellery at her throat or ears or on her fingers.

There was a tiny frown line between her eyebrows as she battled with the coffee machine and, God help him, he wanted to kiss it—the line, not the coffee machine. Although, after the lack of sleep he'd had in the three nights since the gala at the Botanical Garden, it was a close-run thing.

But, most of all, he just wanted to know who this woman he'd spent weeks falling for really was.

And why she'd lied to him.

'So,' he said, when they were finally seated on separate squashy white sofas, either side of the coffee table—which had been stripped of its sewing room accessories. 'What the hell has been going on, Rowan?'

She winced at the harshness of his tone, but he refused to feel guilty about it. He had every right to be angry about being lied to.

Rowan placed her coffee cup on the table— then hurriedly reached into a drawer and pulled out a coaster and put it on that. Now that he knew the truth, he could see how ill at ease she was in this apartment. He'd put it down to an interior designer and home organiser setting everything up without her input. But the truth was, she just didn't belong here—and he couldn't believe it had taken him so long to see it.

Looking up, she caught and held his gaze, her expression open and her eyes clear. Whatever came next, he had faith that it would be the truth.

This time.

'I'm going to tell you everything,' she said evenly. 'The whole story, from start to finish. And when I'm done, well. It's up to you what you do with the information. But I really hope you'll stay and listen to the reasons why I would appreciate it if you could keep my presence here—and my sister's whereabouts—a secret for now. Especially from your brother.'

Oh, he didn't like the sound of that at all.

His brain had been right. This was bad.

'Start talking,' he said. 'And I'll listen.'

CHAPTER NINE

ROWAN WATCHED ELI'S face carefully as she explained the strange sequence of events that had brought them to this moment.

The three days when he'd refused to answer her phone calls had given her plenty of time to figure out what she was going to say. She'd contemplated going down to the Launch offices and confronting him directly, but, given the open-plan nature of the place, she'd thought better of it.

She needed privacy for this conversation, just in case he blew up completely.

She started with an explanation of her own history, and Willow's, and how she'd walked away from her modelling career and the fame that came with it several years ago. She talked about how Willow had always supported and defended her—even though she didn't understand what Rowan was feeling. She talked about the anxiety attacks, the pressure, her mother, and the summer locked away in that London townhouse learning to sew.

Eli nodded thoughtfully. 'That explains a lot. But not why you're here and Willow is... Where *is* Willow?'

'Rumbelow,' Rowan replied. 'It's a tiny fishing village in England where I live. You'd love it. Well, for a visit.' Because, now she thought about it, she couldn't imagine Eli in Rumbelow. Eli belonged to the city. To the kids he helped, and the society he was born into—even if his role now was more making that society see the problems they'd rather ignore. He was designer suits and swanky hotel bars and events at botanical gardens that felt like magic.

And yes, he was also quiet dinners and a beer while he watched her sew, and holding her hand sitting on the floor through a panic attack.

But that didn't mean he'd fit in back home in the place she loved. If she was out of place here in New York, he'd be just as much so in Rumbelow.

'Rumbelow?' Eli asked, frowning. 'What the hell kind of name is that?'

Rowan sighed. 'I know. Anyway. Back to the story.'

This was the difficult bit, of course. Explaining why Willow had come to her. And, more than that, why Rowan had agreed not just to keep her secret, but also to take part in this masquerade.

She'd decided, lying awake at night, that the only way to tell it was exactly as it had happened.

So she did.

Eli listened in silence, but she could see him going stiller, feel him drawing away with every word she said. By the time she'd reached the end, she was shaking.

'And then I arrived here and found you in her apartment and, well, I guess that was the last straw after a very stressful couple of days.'

He squeezed her hand. When had he started holding her hand? She couldn't even remember, it just felt so right. 'I bet it was.'

Eli took a deep breath, then let it out again, as if he'd thought he had something to say and had forgotten it. Rowan watched him carefully as he processed everything she'd told him.

Finally, he said, 'She's really pregnant?'

'I can show you the ultrasound photo.'

'And it's Ben's baby? For sure?' Rowan gave him a filthy look, and he shook his head.

'Sorry. Of course it is. I just… I have to ask because…'

'Because?' she prompted him when he trailed off.

'A secret for a secret?' Eli said suddenly, sitting up a little straighter and pulling his hand away from hers. 'Not that mine is much of one, really. Most of New York probably knows.'

'Knows what?' Rowan shifted a little in her seat, leaning in towards him.

'That my father—Ben's father—probably wasn't mine.'

Rowan's shock must have shown on her face because he shook his head lightly, a rueful smile playing around his lips. This was old news to him, she supposed, something he'd come to terms with, but still shocking all the same.

'When did you find out?' she asked.

'That's the thing. I always knew there was something different in the way our father treated me compared to Ben. Ben was the golden child, the heir apparent, the one who got all the schooling in the way of the company, the one who went to functions and events with Dad, who met everyone that mattered. And I was the one who was shut outside with his secretary, doing my homework.'

He spoke plainly, evenly, but all the same Rowan couldn't help but imagine a lonely little boy, not understanding why he didn't matter the same way his brother did.

She knew that feeling. The feeling of not measuring up. She'd felt it too, every time she'd started shaking before a fashion show and her mother had snapped at her, wanting to know why she couldn't be more like her sister.

'When I was old enough to notice and mind, I started asking questions. Asking people why my father didn't love me the way he loved Ben,' Eli went on. 'They all told me I was imagining things, that I was making it up.'

'They gaslit you,' Rowan said, softly. 'They lied.'

'Basically, yes,' Eli agreed, his jaw tight. 'That's why I have such…issues with lies, even now.'

And she'd lied to him for weeks about something as fundamental as who she was. No wonder he'd refused to take her calls. The only miracle was that he was here now at all.

'How did you find out the truth?' she asked.

Eli shrugged. 'I'll probably never know for sure—unless Ben agrees to a DNA test, which I doubt. With both my legal parents dead, there's no one to ask. But eventually, as

I grew older, after my mother was gone, people got less careful about what they said when I was around. The gossip mill loves a scandal here in the city, and if the parents were talking about it the kids knew as well, and they weren't afraid to let me know.'

'Did you ever ask your father?'

'What was the point? He'd only have lied too.' Eli looked away from her, reaching out for his coffee. It had to be stone cold by now, but he drank the remaining dregs anyway.

'Would you like another?' She reached for his cup, but he shook his head.

'No. I need to get going.' He was already standing before he'd finished the sentence.

Rowan stood too. 'Going? Where? We still need to talk about—'

'We've talked,' Eli interrupted. 'You've told me the truth, and I appreciate it. But now I have to go.'

Oh, Rowan had a really bad feeling about this. 'And do what?'

'And tell Ben the truth.'

'Eli, you can't!' Rowan's plaintive cry caught at his heart, but he turned towards the door anyway.

He couldn't let a pretty face distract him

from doing what he knew was right. Even if Rowan was so much more than that.

'My brother has a right to know he's going to be a father.' For all he knew, his own, real, father had never been given that chance. He wouldn't be the one to deprive Ben of it.

'I absolutely agree.' Rowan put a hand on his arm to stop him and met his gaze with wide, honest eyes. 'I told Willow the same thing. It was part of our agreement for me coming here.'

'Then why are you trying to stop me?'

'Because Willow also has a right to figure out what she wants to do before talking to Ben,' she said, and Eli's heart contracted.

'She's thinking about not keeping the baby? Rowan, she *has* to talk to Ben before she makes that decision.'

Rowan shook her head. 'That decision, at least, is already made. She's keeping it.'

Relief flooded through him. While he fully supported a woman's right to choose, if it came to him keeping that knowledge from his brother for the rest of his life, he knew he'd never have been able to live with the guilt.

'But if she's keeping it, what else is there to think about?'

'She and Ben aren't together right now, remember?' Rowan pointed out. 'In fact, he's been off swanning on his yacht with another woman.'

'True.' Eli let her tug him down to the sofa again, and this time she sat beside him, close enough to touch.

He *could* touch now, he realised. If he wanted. Because she wasn't his brother's girl any more.

Just the woman who'd been lying to him.

'Willow just wants some time to figure out how it will all work. I don't think…they're not going to get back together this time, Eli. She wants to go this alone. But obviously Ben will need to be involved, if he wants to be, and I think Willow wants to decide for herself what she wants that to look like, before he comes in and steamrollers all over her and dictates the way it will work.'

'Ben wouldn't—' Eli stopped. Because he suspected Willow was right. Ben absolutely would.

He was a lot like their father, that way. He saw the way he thought things should be done, and demanded that was what happened.

'How long?' he asked instead.

Rowan shook her head. 'I'm not sure. But it can't be much longer, I don't think. I told her I need to be back in Rumbelow before too long, anyway. I've got dress commissions to get started on. I'm doing what I can from here, dealing with emails and sketching designs, but it's kind of a hands-on process, you know?'

'So I saw.' He thought of Rowan spending all that time with Kelly, perfecting her dream dress—then standing back and watching her glow on the night of the gala.

Maybe that was the clearest sign that the woman he'd fallen for over the past few weeks was Rowan, not Willow. Willow was used to standing in the limelight, the centre of attention, while Rowan hid away in her ridiculously named fishing village.

The fact that *Willow* was now the one in hiding...maybe that was something to think about too. That she felt she couldn't be in the same city as Ben while figuring this out.

What did that say about his brother, and their relationship?

Eli pushed the thought aside. Ben was his brother and, despite their differences, he still loved and trusted him—the same way Willow clearly trusted Rowan. Ben deserved the truth—and Rowan deserved to go back to living her own life again.

Except then she'll leave New York.

The thought stopped him in his mental tracks.

Somehow, he hadn't made that connection yet—that Rowan wouldn't be staying. Perhaps because it felt so much like she belonged here, with him.

But she didn't, did she? The first day she'd arrived she'd had an anxiety attack—although, to be fair, that was mostly his fault. But still. He could recount numerous occasions over the past few weeks where she'd stepped outside to get air, or where her smile had seemed too tight to be real. She found this city hard to navigate, and he'd known that and ignored it.

She didn't want to be here.

And he really didn't want her to leave.

But how could he ask her to stay?

'So another couple of weeks, at most?' His voice came out a little hoarse, and she looked at him strangely. He cleared his throat. 'Until you swap back and Willow tells Ben the truth?'

'I guess.' She looked down at her hands. 'I really should be getting back soon. And she'll be…pretty pregnant by then. At least halfway, I think. She'll need to have a plan.'

'Right.' For a moment, his head swam with an image of Rowan pregnant, and he swallowed, hard.

'Do you think…could you just wait until then, to tell Ben, I mean?' Rowan fixed him with her pleading gaze. 'Just give her the chance to do it herself.'

'If he ever finds out I knew before he did…' He loved his brother, but he didn't love his temper. Ben hated being the last to know anything. And this…yeah, he'd be furious. Rightly so too.

'Why would he?' Rowan asked reasonably. 'He doesn't even know we've been spending time together, right?'

'Right.' And they needed to keep it that way.

Before, he'd kept his connection with the woman he'd thought was Willow a secret from his brother because of the guilt he felt about his feelings for her. Now, when he was free to feel however he liked about Rowan, he had a new reason to feel guilty. A worse one, in lots of ways.

He should walk out of there right now, find his brother, and tell him the truth.

But he already knew he wasn't going to. Not because Willow needed more time.

Because Rowan had asked him to.

'Two weeks,' he said. 'That's all I can promise. And in return…'

'Anything,' Rowan said quickly, already beaming.

'You have to…' What? What could he ask of her, really? 'Help me out at the Castaway Café this week.'

'Deal.' Her smile faded and she gripped his hand tightly. 'Thank you, Eli.'

'It's just two weeks,' he said.

But he didn't know if he was reassuring her or himself.

The relief that Rowan felt at Eli's agreeing to keep Willow's secret was short-lived. Because when she called to tell her twin about their new deadline for getting things sorted, Willow dropped another unexpected bomb into her life.

'You need me to *what?*' Rowan squealed. 'You said I wouldn't have to do any of that!'

The deal was that she'd come to New York and be seen around the place so Ben wouldn't get suspicious. No photoshoots, no fashion shows. That was the *deal*.

'I know, I know,' Willow said apologetically. 'But this is for a friend, and I owe her.

It's only a little—like, absolutely tiny—preview of her new collection. That's *all*. There'll hardly be anyone in the room even watching, Rowan, I promise.'

That wasn't the point, though, and Willow knew it as well as Rowan.

The point was that the last time she'd tried to set foot on a catwalk, she couldn't.

Their mother had been furious, but Willow had talked her down. Convinced her to just let Rowan do the photoshoots while Willow handled the shows. Nobody was happy about the arrangement—everyone wanted the identical twins walking down that runway together, for maximum impact—but Willow had stood firm, which meant Rowan had been able to too.

Otherwise, she was pretty sure she'd have had a major meltdown on camera at a New York Fashion Week show, and that wouldn't have been good for anybody.

But now Willow was the one asking her to step onto that catwalk again.

'I don't know if I can, Will,' she said softly.

'*I* know,' Willow replied. 'You've grown so much since then, Ro. I think you can do anything. I saw the photos online of you at that gala at the Botanical Gardens—you were glowing. There were cameras and hundreds of people and it didn't faze you one bit, did it?'

'Well…' Rowan wasn't sure that was completely true. But she *had* managed the evening, hadn't she? She'd just pretended she was Willow when anyone she didn't know spoke to her or looked at her and—

Oh. Maybe that was all she had to do at the fashion show too.

Could she do that?

If Willow had asked her at the start of this switch, she'd have said no. But now…

'Maybe,' she said slowly. 'Maybe I can do it.'

'I know you can,' Willow reassured her. 'Piece of cake.'

But Rowan's hands were still trembling as she handed over plates to the kids at the Castaway Café the next day—and Eli noticed.

After she almost dropped a tray full of hot-dogs, he steered her away from the counter and into the back room, his hand warm at her back, and just the scent of him was somehow reassuring.

'What's wrong?' he asked, once the door was shut behind them and they were alone. 'Has something happened?'

'Willow called yesterday. She needs me to

do a small fashion show. As her.' There, just the simple truth. It definitely sounded less terrifying when she said it out loud.

Okay, it didn't. But she was pretending it did, anyway.

Eli didn't fall for it, though. 'And you're freaking out. Understandably.'

'I'm not freaking out,' she snapped. Eli gave her a look, and she slumped down to sit in the ancient armchair by the window. 'Okay, maybe a bit.'

'I can't believe she asked you to do it.' Eli paced in front of the door, his hands thrust deep in his pockets. 'I mean, she knows what happened last time you had to do that. You told me—it's what set off your biggest panic attack ever, and made you leave modelling in the first place! I thought your deal was that you wouldn't have to do any of this stuff?'

'It was. But…things come up. And this is a favour to a friend. And…'

'And?' Eli pressed, when she trailed off.

Rowan sat forward, her forearms resting against her thighs, and focused hard on the door handle on the other side of the room, thinking.

'Rowan?' Eli said, when she stayed silent.

'I think… I think this might have been part of Willow's plan all along,' she said finally.

'You mean she got pregnant just so you'd have to come to New York and do a fashion show again for the first time in years?' The incredulity in Eli's voice was plain. 'I think that might be pushing it a bit.'

'No, of course I don't mean that.' Except… in a small way, she did. Sitting back, she tried to explain. 'You realise that Ben hasn't been near her apartment, the whole time I've been there?'

'Well, no. Because he was…'

'Off on a yacht with that other woman, yes,' Rowan finished. 'And Willow must have known he'd do that. From what I understand, it's his modus operandi.'

Eli winced, obviously not enjoying thinking of his brother as that kind of man. 'I wouldn't know. But…yeah, perhaps.'

'Maybe it was useful for her to have me here, being seen, so no one—especially the media—would start speculating about where she'd gone,' Rowan continued, still thinking aloud. 'But it wasn't exactly essential. She could have hidden out in Rumbelow with me, and if anyone got suspicious we could have said *I* was the one who was pregnant, and that was why she was there.'

'That would have been a lot to ask of you,' Eli said.

'And coming to New York wasn't?' Rowan shook her head. 'No, I get that this worked out well for what Willow needed—time and space away from Ben, without him or anyone else wondering where she was. But it was kind of extreme, don't you think? This whole sister swap scheme?'

'You think she had another reason too?'

Oh, Rowan was almost certain she had. After all, she knew Willow. And Willow always had at least a dozen reasons for every decision she made.

'I think she wanted to get me out of my comfort zone, and back into the real world again.'

As soon as she said it aloud, she knew it was true.

And from Eli's face, he did too. 'And you're… How are you feeling about that?'

Rowan couldn't think about feelings just yet. She was still on logistics, and trying to read her sister's mind from across an ocean. 'I think she thought that if I came here I'd find my confidence again. I don't think she imagined I'd suddenly want to get back into modelling—that was never really me, anyway. But maybe she thought I'd retreated and hidden myself away a bit *too* much, so this was her way of forcing me to face up to that. While also conveniently giving her everything she needed too.' That would be very Willow.

'Suddenly I'm understanding why your sister and my brother were together for so long,' he said dryly.

'Given what I know of your brother, that's not exactly complimentary to my sister.'

Eli shook his head. 'He's not a bad man. He just…he has that same sort of mind. The sort that sees a situation and finds a path of action that addresses half a dozen problems all at the same time. It's what has made him so successful in his business. And his personal life, to a point.'

'I can see that, I suppose.' The only problem with that plan of action, in Rowan's experience, was that it didn't always solve all the problems equally well. And sometimes it forgot about the people at the heart of it.

'Of course, sometimes he just manages to screw up all the things at the same time,' Eli went on. 'Like losing Willow, not knowing she's pregnant and being stuck on a yacht with the most vacant woman of all time.'

That surprised a laugh from her, and Rowan relaxed back into her seat, thinking hard.

'So, what are you going to do?' Eli asked. 'Now you've figured this out?'

'I'm going to see if she's right,' Rowan said slowly. 'If I really am ready to do this.'

It was a risk, of course. But she'd already come so far.

Why not take it the whole way?

CHAPTER TEN

ELI HAD NEVER attended a fashion show before—he'd never had any desire or need to either. But wild horses wouldn't have kept him away from today's.

As Willow had promised, it really was only a small affair, with just a few rows of chairs filled with people who all seemed to know each other. The catwalk jutted out into the room between the seats and long black curtains hid whatever was going on behind the scenes from sight.

Eli took a seat to one side, as close as he could get to those curtains, his phone gripped tightly in his hand. He hadn't been allowed backstage—and Rowan had told him he'd only make her more nervous anyway—but he wanted, no, needed, to be close at hand. Just in case.

His phone was on silent, of course, so he stared at the screen, waiting to see if it would light up with a desperate plea from Rowan to come and help her. What if she had another panic attack? Or just couldn't do it and needed him to drive the getaway car?

'I have techniques and methods to deal with this, Eli,' she'd told him in the car on the way over. 'I've learned a lot about how to manage my anxiety since the last time I was on a catwalk. I'm not the same person I was back then—and, even more importantly, my mother isn't there to be unbearable about everything either.'

It was still a risk, though, as far as Eli was concerned. Not just because of how Rowan might react to being backstage at a fashion show again, but because the designer was a friend of Willow's. A real friend would surely realise that the woman wearing her designs *wasn't* Willow at all. Wouldn't she?

Rowan hadn't thought so, when he'd suggested it in the car. 'She'll be too busy flapping about the show going smoothly to notice. As long as we don't hang around afterwards we'll be fine. And Willow has already told her she'll have to make a sharp exit because of another commitment.'

So now here he was, just sitting there, willing his heart to slow down, more nervous than if he was the one preparing to parade about in the latest fashions for an audience.

The phone in his hand buzzed, and he looked down to see a message.

Stop gripping your phone so tight; you'll break it.

He smiled, even as it buzzed again.

And stop glaring at the catwalk. If the wind changes your face will stay like that.

That made him laugh out loud, much to the concern of the people sitting around him.

Eli looked up to try and find where Rowan was watching him from, but saw only the flutter of a curtain. At least he knew she was doing okay so far.

The lights dimmed, and the small crowd settled, as music started over the speakers. Eli sucked in a deep breath, and had to remind himself to let it go again as he waited for Rowan to appear on the catwalk.

She wasn't the first model to appear, or even the second or third. Eli suspected she was the surprise extra appearance on the runway to win over the audience—and, sure enough, she was the last one out. Afterwards,

Eli couldn't have said what any of the others had been wearing, but the outfit Rowan had been dressed in would be burned in his memory for all time.

Apparently, chain mail was a thing this season, or maybe Joan of Arc chic, Eli wasn't sure. Fashion wasn't his specialist subject. But the diaphanous white fabric that clung to Rowan's body, anchored only by strips of fine silver chains, was something he was willing to study at great length.

Preferably while removing it. With his teeth.

Hell, she couldn't be wearing *anything* under that, or it would show through. All he could see was the rosy glow of her skin peeking through the fabric…

There was a murmur of excitement as Rowan made her way down the catwalk, hips swaying gently, her gaze focused straight ahead, a Mona Lisa non-smile playing around her lips. Her hair had been slicked back into a low knot at the base of her neck, her face mostly bare of make-up except for a shimmery finish on her cheeks and collarbones.

She looked beautiful. Ethereal. Untouchable.

But God, he wanted to touch her.

'How the hell did she get Willow Harper to

appear here?' someone behind him asked in an astonished whisper. Eli glanced back just in time to see their companion shrug their confusion too.

Designer friend or not, Eli suspected Willow would normally have turned this down, if the woman up there in the breathtaking dress really *had* been Willow. This must be another of Rowan's sister's ploys—a way to get her sister to dip her toe back into the world she'd left behind, without being too terrified.

When Rowan had first mentioned her suspicions about Willow's motives, he'd had to swallow down the anger they raised. Who was she to trick Rowan into doing *anything* she was uncomfortable with? Willow had used her twin's love for her to force her into a situation she didn't want to be in, and that was not okay.

Except if she hadn't, he might never have met her. Never have fallen for her as hard as he had—something he'd basically given up denying even to himself at this point.

It still didn't make it okay.

But watching Rowan up there, owning that catwalk, reclaiming a life she'd walked away from in fear and anxiety…it was hard to stay angry with Willow right in that moment.

The show reached its conclusion before Eli had managed to reconcile his thoughts on the matter, and he joined in the rapturous applause as all the models—and the designer—took a final bow on the catwalk.

'I heard Willow is designing gowns herself now,' he heard someone say as the audience got to their feet and headed towards the drinks and nibbles set up in the next room. 'Maybe that's why she agreed to do this show—contacts are everything.'

Another person scoffed. 'It's not like she doesn't have enough of those by herself. If I were her, I'd be more worried about having the *talent*. It's a long jump from wearing clothes to designing them.'

'I don't know,' their companion said. Eli turned towards the voices in time to see one of them showing the other their phone screen. 'Says here she designed this dress for some woman at a charity gala event…not too shabby.' Were they talking about *Kelly's* dress? How had *that* got out on the internet?

The same way everything did, he supposed. They'd had an official photographer, but plenty of other people had been taking photos on their phones and posting them to social media. Kelly could even have put it up there herself, and it wasn't as if they'd told her not to mention Willow was the designer. Even if they had, everyone in the Launch offices knew 'Willow' had been working on it.

Maybe the real surprise was that it hadn't got out sooner.

The other person took the phone and studied it. 'That's not bad, actually. Although if she's planning on making a niche out of designing dresses for the imperfectly proportioned the internet will pile on for sure.'

They wandered away before Eli could hear any more of their conversation, and he headed over to find Rowan to make their swift getaway, still thinking.

When she emerged, at the back door as planned, Rowan was back in her jeans, T-shirt and jacket, her hair up in a ponytail, and only the slight shimmer on her cheeks a sign that she'd ever worn anything else at all.

She'd done it. She'd walked down that catwalk like a pro—and, more importantly, she'd faced her demons and she'd won. And he was so damn proud of her he could hardly see straight.

'Did I look okay?' she asked as he wrapped her up into a tight hug.

'Magnificent,' he murmured against her shoulder. 'You were…you were incredible.'

She pulled away, blushing slightly. 'Thanks. So…uh… I suppose we should get out of here before someone stops us and drags us back for the party. What do you want to do now?'

'I am taking you out,' he told her. 'For a celebratory New York tour.'

It wasn't what he *wanted* to do, exactly. But their relationship, such as it was, hadn't reached that stage yet for everything he wanted to do. So, for now, they'd stay in public, where he wouldn't be tempted to rush them to that next level. There was still a lot of trust to build up between them first.

Not *too* public, though. Places where Ben wouldn't even think to go, and it wouldn't get back to him that they'd been out together.

Maybe Rowan should wear a hat or something, just in case.

'Sounds great,' Rowan said, beaming. She was bouncing on the toes of her tennis shoes, and he knew the adrenaline had to still be racing through her body. Getting out and active would help her burn that off too. And in her street clothes she looked so much more like *her* than her more famous sister. Odds were she might not even be recognised at all, if they were careful.

Somewhere, a door banged. Rowan's eyes widened, and he grabbed her arm to lead her to where he'd parked.

'I don't suppose you get to keep the see-through dress with the chains, do you?' he asked casually, as they headed to the car.

She laughed. 'You liked that one, huh? Well, sorry to disappoint, but I had to give it back. Maybe I could make something similar, though. Just for wearing at home…'

'I would not object to that,' Eli replied, grinning.

'Good to know.'

Rowan had a feeling that Eli's idea of a tour of New York City wouldn't be in any of the tourist guidebooks, and she suspected the reason for that had more to do with avoiding his brother and anyone who might recognise her and report back than anything else.

'You already saw all the obvious stuff when you were living here as a teen, right?' He tucked her hand through his arm as he led her along the pavement away from where they'd left the car. 'So I figure we'll do some things I bet you *didn't* see.'

They stopped outside a large red brick building with classic black metal fire escapes down the side. Rowan squinted up at the sign. 'The Tenement Museum?'

Eli nodded. 'It's my favourite New York museum. Come on. I've booked us on a tour of the apartments of nineteenth-century immigrants, and it's about to start!'

Rowan couldn't help but grin at his enthusiasm. Of course this was his favourite museum.

An hour later, she had to admit he'd been right; the tour was fascinating.

The only slightly distracting thing was the way her phone kept beeping with new emails, voicemails and messages—all of them forwarded from Willow, and all of them asking for details of her bespoke gowns. Which didn't exist.

Rowan switched her phone off and concentrated on learning about the lives of immigrant Americans in the nineteenth century instead.

After their tour, Eli dropped her home and, when she invited him in, shook his head. 'Not yet.'

'Yet?' Yet implied that one day he'd come in again—and with purpose.

Eli nodded, then ducked his head to touch his lips to hers. Surprised, Rowan gasped, and Eli deepened the kiss with a groan.

The sound reverberated through her body, making every nerve-ending tingle, and her blood heat. Her hands reached around to hold him closer, until he was pressing her against the door, and she could feel how much he *wanted* to come in…so why wouldn't he?

Suddenly, Eli pulled away, panting. Resting his forehead against hers, he said, 'If I come in now, I don't think I'll be able to leave. Definitely not for a few days. And there's more of my New York I want to show you first.'

'That's the only reason?' Because it didn't feel like it. They only had a couple of weeks left together, and she didn't want to waste a moment.

Eli just gave her a small sad smile, and she knew he wasn't quite ready to trust her that far, not yet. But hopefully soon.

'I just want to know you as *you,* first,' he explained.

And then, with a last burst of self-resolve that, from the expression on his face, might have been physically painful, he was gone. Leaving her breathless against her sister's apartment door, her mind filled with images of what the next few days might have looked like if he wasn't so damned principled.

True to his word, he was back the next morning, ready to take her on an app walking tour from his phone that took them to all the best delis, showcasing international foods from around the world. Once they were stuffed, they visited his favourite second-hand bookshop, where Rowan found a fantastic selection of vintage dress patterns stuffed into a wicker basket at the back.

Then he left her at her apartment door again, with another mind-bending kiss, and the basket full of sewing patterns he'd insisted on buying for her.

With a sigh, Rowan went inside to check the dozen or more messages on her phone.

On the third day, he took her somewhere she hadn't even imagined could exist in New York.

'No, really. How does this city have actual medieval cloisters?'

Eli laughed. 'They're part of the Met Museum,' he explained. 'And they were actually built in 1933, but using medieval European-style architecture. Come on, let's go see if we can find a unicorn.'

'A unicorn?' Rowan echoed as she followed

him through a Gothic chapel. But really, nothing would surprise her at this point.

They *did* find the unicorn—actually a series of unicorn tapestries, but magical enough for Rowan—then took a walk through the cloister gardens.

As her phone buzzed again in her pocket, Eli looked down at it. 'Not going to answer that?'

Rowan shook her head. 'I don't think mobile phones were encouraged in medieval Europe. Just pretend it doesn't exist.'

Eli smiled, but it didn't quite reach his eyes. 'Okay.'

Then she realised—the real reason he kept saying goodbye at her apartment door, even now.

He thought she was keeping something else from him, but she wasn't, not really. She just didn't want to deal with it at all.

Maybe later. Later, she'd tell him about all the requests and commissions, and the interviews Willow kept turning down, and how everyone out there thought that Kelly's dress was *Willow's* work, and she had no idea how she was going to untangle that mess, or if she even wanted to.

Right now, she just wanted to soak in the

peace of the cloister gardens, and imagine a unicorn running through them. Was that so bad?

She leant her head against Eli's shoulder as they walked, arm in arm. 'Thank you for bringing me here,' she murmured.

'Thank you for coming,' Eli replied, and the emotion in his voice told her he wasn't just talking about the Cloisters.

They lingered in the Cloisters a long time. Eli had always loved the place for the quiet, and the space for reflection, and he'd guessed Rowan would too. It hadn't occurred to him until they were there that, living in England, she probably got to see the real thing all the time, if she wanted.

But Rowan had shook her head when he'd suggested it. 'I don't leave Rumbelow much,' she'd explained. 'And there are no medieval cloisters there—just rotting fishing boats!'

He hadn't mentioned it again, but he couldn't help but wonder what was so wonderful about Rumbelow that she never left the place. Or was it more that everything outside it was so terrible—or terrifying?

She'd come to New York, though. Perhaps she was ready for other new adventures too.

Maybe even with him.

After the Cloisters, they headed to Giovanni's—which Eli firmly believed was the best ice cream parlour in the world—and took their cones for a walk through the park.

'It's good,' Rowan admitted after a few mouthfuls. 'But you should come to Rumbelow and try Marco's ice cream.'

'Maybe one day,' Eli replied, even though he couldn't really imagine it. He was a city boy through and through—and the idea that anywhere had better anything than New York was clearly absurd.

As he stole a lick of Rowan's strawberry shortcake cone, her phone buzzed again in her pocket. She reached in and flicked it off, but that didn't stem Eli's curiosity.

She didn't want to talk about whatever was blowing up her phone, that much was clear. But that didn't mean she shouldn't. Eli had a feeling that Rowan was enjoying avoiding reality right now—but that didn't mean it wasn't going to come back and bite them both anyway.

He'd been so determined to spend time getting to know her as *Rowan,* not Willow, before they took things any further, but now he wondered. How much time did they really have?

At some point, they were going to have to have the difficult conversations. Life wasn't all unicorns and ice cream. Unfortunately.

Her phone buzzed yet again, and Rowan gave a heavy sigh.

Eli tugged her arm gently to get her to sit down beside him on the nearest bench, where they could stare out over the other parkgoers.

'You don't have to tell me what's going on that you don't want to answer your phone about,' he said cautiously. He wasn't sure what the right or wrong thing to say was, and the last thing he wanted to do was put his foot in it now. 'But if it would help to talk about it...'

With another sigh, Rowan pulled her phone from her pocket, opened her email app and passed it to him.

Frowning, Eli scrolled through what looked like a screenful of messages from Willow. Until he looked a little closer.

'These are all dress commissions,' he said, still scrolling. 'Or requests for them, at least. People are going to Willow thinking she designed Kelly's dress for the gala?'

'Apparently.' Rowan took the phone back.

'There are voicemails and texts too. Willow's getting pretty fed up of having to forward them all, since I won't answer any of them.'

'Do you think maybe you should?' Eli didn't want to presume. Everything between them was so tenuous and new—a few longing kisses and a distance he kept in place without even fully knowing why. It wasn't his place to decide what she should do or not—it never would be, no matter how close they grew. But if she wanted his advice… 'This sounds like the sort of thing that isn't going to go away in a hurry.'

Rowan sighed. 'It's only because they think it was Willow—that *I* am Willow. Which… I know that was the plan, but this is different. Designing and making bespoke gowns… that's *my* thing, I taught myself how to do it and built up a small business back home making clothes I cared about for people who deserved to feel beautiful. I did that. Not Willow. And now…'

'Now you think people are cashing in on the name and the moment and wanting to get close to a celebrity?' Eli guessed. When she nodded, he eased the phone from her hand again and scrolled through the messages. 'You know, some of these don't even mention Willow's celebrity. They just really, really liked the dress. Look at this one... "As a plus size woman of colour, I can't tell you how much it meant to me to see a bespoke gown like that. To know that I could have clothes that make me feel beautiful just the way I am. I can't afford it yet, but maybe one day! Please keep making the dresses for people like me. I'm saving up!"'

Rowan looked up. 'I didn't... I didn't read them all,' she admitted.

Or any of them, Eli was willing to bet.

'I don't think they're only interested because they think you're Willow,' Eli murmured. 'Just like I wasn't.'

She gave a watery chuckle at that. 'You really wished I *wasn't* Willow for most of the time we've known each other, didn't you?'

'Damn right, I did.' Those days of crippling guilt about lusting after his brother's girl had now been replaced with the guilt of lying to him, but knowing that Rowan was *Rowan* was still a relief. 'Looks like wishes can come true, after all.'

She met his gaze, and what he saw there felt like everything that had been building inside him over the past weeks.

Finally, they were on the same page.

'You should respond to some of those messages,' he said, his voice sounding hoarse even to his own ears.

'What's the point? I'll be going home soon, anyway. I won't be here to make the dresses.'

The words hung between them, and Eli wondered if all the other things she wouldn't be there to do were racing through her head too.

He looked away. 'I should take you home.'

'Right.' She paused, and he couldn't help but sneak a glance up at her. 'Will you come inside this time?'

The wanting in her voice, the heat in her eyes, left him in no doubt of his answer.

'Yes.'

CHAPTER ELEVEN

ROWAN STRETCHED AGAINST the sheets of her sister's bed the next morning, her body pleasantly aching and every muscle relaxed.

Well.

That had been worth waiting for.

She smiled at the curve of Eli's body beside her, the sunlight pouring in and warming his bare skin. He had one hand flung out towards her, the other tucked against his chest, as if he was both giving away his heart and holding hers close and safe at the same time.

She knew how he felt.

Last night had been incredible. Turned out, all that pent-up longing and unconsummated desire was good for one thing—when they'd finally given in, they hadn't held back. From the moment they'd stumbled through the door, already kissing, it had been a race to see who could get the other naked first. Then she'd fallen onto the bed and he'd lowered himself over her and…

Maybe she should wake him up for another round.

Eli gave a light snore and burrowed deeper into the mattress, and she abandoned the idea with a fond smile. Apparently the three rounds last night would have to suffice for now.

She could live with that.

As long as they were exploring each other's bodies, they weren't exploring the far trickier subject of what happened next. When Willow came back to New York, and she headed home to Rumbelow.

The thought ruined the warm and hazy morning-after feeling, so Rowan slipped out from between the sheets without waking Eli, to go find some coffee. Spotting his white shirt on the floor—and remembering stripping it from him and humming her approval as she examined the broad, lightly muscled shoulders underneath with her mouth—she smiled. Maybe, just for this morning, she could be that girl in the movie. Living in New York, having incredible sex with a new, gorgeous and considerate lover—who also made it his life's mission to care for the less fortunate. And, most critically in this moment, gliding around a sunlit penthouse apartment in Manhattan on a lazy morning wearing nothing but her lover's expensively tailored white shirt.

She was a tall woman, but Eli was even taller, and the tails of his shirt covered the very top of her thighs at least when she slipped it on. It wasn't something she'd wear out in public, but for the very limited plans she had for the rest of the morning it would do just fine. She fastened the most crucial buttons and headed out into the kitchen to wrestle with the coffee-maker, already imagining Eli's expression when he finally woke and came to find her.

She'd *almost* managed to make a latte, and was about to tackle a plain americano for Eli, when she heard the front door to the apartment open.

Willow. Rowan spun around, expecting to see her sister, fresh off the plane and here to tell her it was time to go home.

Instead, she found herself face to face with a man she only knew from photos. Magazine shots with Willow. And that family photo on Eli's desk.

Ben.

Oh, this was not good. At least Eli was still in bed. If she could just get rid of him without Eli waking up, maybe this would still be a good morning after all.

But her chest was already tightening, and she had to focus hard on her breathing to even get any words out at all.

'What are you doing here?'

'What, I can't come visit my girlfriend when I get back to town?' Ben asked, an amused smile on his face.

'We broke up. Remember?'

He rolled his eyes. 'Like that's never happened before. Listen, I've got this awards dinner next week. Want to patch things up in time to appear on my arm in all the glossy magazines?'

Rowan swallowed. What would Willow say?

Well, based on past evidence, she'd probably say yes—she always had before. But that was before there was the baby to consider. And since Rowan *wasn't* Willow, she could make the right choice here, on her sister's behalf.

And the fact that his brother was naked in her bedroom had practically nothing to do with it.

'No, Ben. I don't want to patch things up. I told you, things are over this time. For real. I'm not playing these games any more.'

Wow. That sounded good, even to her own ears. Strong and determined. Exactly the way she wished she'd been able to talk to her mother, when she'd decided to leave modelling behind for good.

Back then, she'd been too scared, too damaged. She'd stolen away in the middle of the night without so much as a note, and left Willow to explain things for her.

Maybe it was appropriate that she was here now, to do the same for her twin.

It felt…right. It felt like closure.

Ben, however, didn't appear to feel the same. His pleasant façade fell away, and his expression twisted into something ugly and entitled.

'What the hell are you doing lately, Willow?' He stalked across the room towards her, and Rowan backed up against the counter instinctively. Her sister had said that Ben had never hurt her physically, but that didn't mean he wasn't still damn intimidating when he wanted to be. 'Designing dresses instead of modelling them? Leaving me high and dry? What's it all about? Is our arrangement not working for you any more?'

Rowan swallowed, trying to get her throat to open enough to answer, but Ben's focus suddenly shifted away from her and over to his left.

To where the bedroom door had just opened.

Oh, help.

Eli stood, mussed and still half asleep, wearing nothing but his boxer shorts, in her bedroom doorway. Even Rowan had to admit that really didn't look good.

'Ben?' Eli blinked a few times, and then his eyes widened as he awoke to the reality of the situation. 'Wait, we can explain this.'

No, they really couldn't. Not without giving away Willow's secret anyway.

Fortunately, Ben didn't seem in a mood to listen to his brother.

Turning on Rowan again, he pressed her up against the counter, his snarling face too close to hers. She gripped the edge of the counter and focused on her breathing. Willow wouldn't have a panic attack at his behaviour, and neither would she. He was all hot air and no substance.

His brother, however, was the opposite. And he was right there if she needed him.

She could sense how much he wanted to come and save her, but he held back, waiting for a sign from her. She didn't give it.

'If you wanted my attention, Willow, you

know how to get it—on your knees,' Ben purred. 'You didn't have to sleep with the runt of the family to win me back.'

How can he talk to her that way?

In that moment, Eli wasn't sure he even recognised his brother. The big brother he'd looked up to, admired, all these years…he would never have spoken to a woman, or to anyone, like that.

Except… Eli had been on the wrong end of Ben's sharp tongue before. He knew his brother's temper of old. He'd never imagined he'd speak to a woman that way—but why not? He cheated on them, said things about them behind their backs—so why not to their faces too?

He'd just wanted to believe the best of his brother, the only family he had left. He'd hoped that Ben was a good man, under all the conditioning their father had put him through. He'd wanted to believe that Ben could choose to be a better man, now their father was gone.

But that hope had fled now, and he finally saw the man his brother truly was before him.

Bile rising in his throat, Eli started towards Ben, determined to rip him away from Rowan, but the calm expression on her face stopped him. She had this under control, and she wouldn't appreciate him bursting in like a knight in shining armour.

Sure enough, Rowan let go of the counter, placed her hands on Ben's chest and pushed. Surprised, he stumbled backwards a few paces, staring at her.

'I don't want you back, Ben,' she said firmly. 'We're done. And nothing between me and Eli has anything to do with you at all.'

One day, probably soon, Willow would have to explain all this to Ben. Eli suspected that would be one hell of a conversation.

Ben looked between the two of them slowly, before settling his gaze on Eli. 'Oh, I see what this is. Tired of trying to live up to my legend in the business world, you thought you'd take on my sloppy seconds instead, huh? Well, brother, I can tell you now, she's too much woman for you to handle.'

Eli gritted his teeth. 'That's not what this is.' If they could just tell him the truth... He looked towards Rowan for guidance, but she shook her head subtly.

Unfortunately, Ben caught it. 'Oh, what's that? Keeping secrets are we—more than the fact you're screwing around behind my back in the first place? I wonder what they could be...'

He turned back to Rowan, obviously assuming she was the easier target. 'What's my little brother been telling you, then? Business secrets? What do you think you know?'

Eli frowned. 'I don't know what you're talking about. I haven't been telling her anything.'

'I want to hear it from her.' Reaching out, Ben grabbed her arm, and Rowan flinched.

And that was all he could take. 'Get off her.' He wrenched his brother away from her, then covered her with his own body against the counter as he checked she was okay.

'I'm fine, Eli,' she said, but her voice was shaking.

'We have to tell him, Rowan,' he whispered.

But not quietly enough.

'Rowan?' Ben echoed, confusion in his voice. Then he repeated it with more certainty. 'Rowan! You're not Willow at all, are you? Well, that makes more sense.' He pushed a hand against Eli's shoulder, but Eli stood his ground. 'Couldn't bag the real thing, so you nailed the sister instead. *Now* I get it.'

It was almost more than Eli could bear. Spinning around so that Rowan was behind him, he faced down his brother. 'You get *nothing.* You don't understand anything here.

And neither do I. How could you speak to her that way? The woman you're supposed to love? The—' He broke off sharply as Rowan dug her nails into his arm.

Oh, God, he'd been about to say *the mother of your child.* They might have given away Rowan's identity, but it was definitely up to Willow to tell Ben about the baby.

'What the hell do you care how I speak to my woman?'

'She's not *your* woman,' Rowan snapped, stepping out from behind Eli before he could stop her. 'She's her own person, and she's chosen to be a long way away from you.'

'Where is she?' Ben demanded, zeroing in on Rowan again.

'There is nothing in this world that could make me tell you that,' she replied calmly.

'And you, *brother?*' Ben spat the word. 'I suppose you're keeping her secret too?'

'I am.'

A slow, sly smile spread across Ben's face. 'Then there must be a very good reason for that. I mean, why else would she go to all this trouble? Sending you here to pretend to be her. No, there's something going on she doesn't want me to know about. And that means I'm *definitely* going to find out. I don't need either of you to tell me.' He turned and covered the floor to the door in long strides. 'But first, I've got a board meeting to attend. Something that you're clearly too busy to make a priority.'

And with a last, satisfied smile at Eli, Ben walked out of the door.

But he left behind a feeling in Eli's gut that something was very wrong.

Rowan slumped back against the counter as the door swung shut behind Ben.

'Well, that could have gone worse. Somehow.' Right now, it was hard to imagine a way in which it *could* have been more of a disaster, but she was sure there was one. Probably.

'There's something else going on,' Eli said, sounding distracted. 'I don't know what, but that wasn't the brother I know. And why was he so desperate to find Willow if he doesn't even know about the baby? No, there's something else at play here.'

'Like what?' Rowan asked. As far as she could see, the only real mystery was why on earth Willow would have dated that jackass in the first place.

'I don't know.' Eli turned to her, running a hand through his hair. He was still only wearing his boxers, she realised with a smile. Although the mood from that morning—or last night—was well and truly shattered. 'But I need to find out what.'

Rowan frowned. There was something more to this. 'What aren't you telling me?' They'd had enough secrets between them already— okay, mostly hers. But it was time to try something new. Honesty.

Eli paused and for a moment she thought he wasn't going to tell her. That he'd lie, or spin a line.

But this was Eli and so, when he spoke, she knew it was the truth.

'The way he was acting then—towards you and even towards me—I've never seen Ben quite like that. He has a temper, but that…he sounded totally desperate. On the edge. I've never seen that before. And I hope you know that if I'd *ever* seen him behave like that towards your sister—or any woman—I'd have called him out, done *something*.'

'I know that,' Rowan murmured. 'I know you.'

It was true, she realised, even as she said the words. She did know him. They'd only been in each other's lives for a handful of weeks, but she *knew* him. The heart and soul and bones of him.

And she was pretty sure he knew her too. Better than anyone except Willow ever had. In some ways, even better than her.

Under other circumstances, the revelation would have been a good thing—something to fill her with light and happiness and possibility for the future.

As it was, all she could think about was what she was going to have to say goodbye to, soon.

Maybe he'd come back to Rumbelow with her. Not to stay, but for a while. Maybe they could have some more time to figure all this out, at least. And she'd like to show him Marco's ice cream shack on the edge of the beach. Give his big city parlour some competition.

It was a flicker of hope, at least.

But Eli wasn't finished.

'He was… It was like being in the room with my father all over again.' He shook his head. 'Something must have happened.'

'Like finding his girlfriend and brother in bed together?' Rowan suggested. Eli himself had said that the idea of someone else touching her would drive him insane, hadn't he?

Eli wasn't convinced. 'He knew you weren't

Willow soon enough. And he'd been off with someone else since they split up, anyway. No, the way he spoke to you, when he thought you *were* her…that wasn't love. That wasn't anything beyond a frustration that a convenient business relationship no longer worked the way he wanted it to.'

Rowan couldn't argue with that; she'd got exactly the same impression. Ben didn't want Willow back because he loved her, but because she was convenient. She looked good on his arm, gave the right message. That he was a successful, attractive businessman who could have any woman he wanted—but also one in a stable, long-term relationship with one of the world's most beautiful women.

He'd been happy to give that impression up though, not so long ago. Happy to be filmed with another woman on a yacht. Was that part of it?

Investors didn't want a playboy; they wanted someone reliable at the helm. Was that why he was so eager to get Willow back?

She glanced at the troubled expression on Eli's face. 'You think it's something to do with the business?'

'The board meeting he was rushing off

to... He told me a while ago I didn't need to attend.'

'Do you usually?'

'No,' Eli admitted. 'Ben doesn't like me meddling with the family business, and I'm only a shareholder really, not an employee. Well, technically, I'm supposed to be on the board of directors, but it never seemed to mean much. My focus was on Launch, so I always left the family business to Ben.'

'So if you don't normally go to the meetings anyway, why did he feel the need to tell you again not to bother going to this one?' Rowan asked.

'That's what I'm wondering.' Eli met her gaze and gave her an apologetic smile. 'I think I have to go. I need to find out what's happening.'

Rowan nodded. 'I understand. Besides... I need to pack.' Ben knew the truth now. She had to get to Willow and Rumbelow before he did.

And, just like that, any small part of the bubble they'd built around themselves the night before that had survived Ben's arrival, disappeared.

Reality was firmly back in charge.

Rowan didn't think she liked it.

CHAPTER TWELVE

ELI REGRETTED LEAVING Rowan the moment the apartment door swung shut behind him. But the relief on the other board members' faces when he arrived at the company offices told him he'd made the right choice.

'Nice to see you decided to show your face for this one, at least.' Eli's godfather, Jeremiah, collared him the moment he entered the meeting room, dragging him off to one side before the other board members could talk to him.

'Where's Ben?' Eli asked, scanning the room. He'd left Willow's apartment before Eli—long before him, by the time Eli had showered and dressed and kissed Rowan goodbye. And left her dragging her suitcase out from under the bed, although he couldn't think about that part now.

'Oh, he'll be watching and waiting until we're all here, making sure we know he's the one in charge by showing up late.' Jeremiah waved a hand. 'I don't want to talk about him. I want to talk about you. Finally taking an interest in the family business, are we?'

'I barely have a *financial* interest in the company,' Eli reminded him. 'Everything important was left to Ben, remember?'

His godfather sighed heavily at that. 'You got short shrift, that's for sure. Whatever your father suspected…you were his son, and he didn't always make you feel that way. That was wrong of him, and you have to believe I told him so, often. But you were your mother's son too—there's so damn much of your mother in you, and I think that hurt him more than anything. Seeing that.'

Eli opened his mouth to respond, but Jeremiah put up a hand to stop him.

'I'm not making excuses for him,' he went on. 'The man was my friend for a lot of years, and I watched him change, as he grew older. I've been watching your brother change too, and you haven't been here to see it.'

Guilt pinged in Eli's chest. He wasn't his brother's keeper, he knew that. But Ben was still his brother, whatever the differences between them. If there was something going on with him, he *should* have been there.

'What's happening here today, Jeremiah?' he asked.

The older man shook his head. 'We'll see, when Ben arrives. A lot of it depends on him, and his attitude, I suspect. But if he carries on the way he has been…'

'I don't know what you expect me to do, though,' Eli said. 'I don't have a controlling share of the company. I don't have any influence here—most of the shareholders barely know me.'

'And that's something you're going to need to do something about.' Jeremiah put an arm around Eli's shoulders. 'Every leader needs someone to keep them in check. To remind them that they're not lord of all they survey—they're there to do what's right. For your father, it was your mom—and once she was gone, well, that's when the wheels started to come off the whole thing. For Ben… I don't think he's ever found that person. There was that supermodel he was seeing, but I never got the impression she had the kind of influence over him she needed.' He gave Eli a sly look. 'Plus, I think I saw her on *your* arm more recently, didn't I?'

'That was her twin sister,' Eli muttered, but Jeremiah was already moving on.

'The point is, Ben needs that someone. And

if he can't find them himself, you're going to have to step up and do it for him. Be his reality check. His conscience. I have a feeling you'd be good at it.'

'What if Ben doesn't want that, though?' Eli asked. 'He tried to keep me from even coming to this meeting, you know.'

Jeremiah sighed. 'What it comes down to is, it's still your name over the building. I'd think you'd want to make sure that means something. Or doesn't mean the wrong thing, anyway.'

Well. That sounded ominous.

'Is it going to? I saw Ben earlier. He seemed... agitated.'

Jeremiah barked a laugh. 'That's one way to put it. He sees the writing on the wall, then. That's good. That will make things easier. Or at least more interesting.'

Eli wanted to ask *what* it would make interesting, when Ben burst through the doors, still fizzing with the same anger he'd displayed earlier. He scowled when he spotted Eli, but didn't acknowledge him any further.

'Right then,' Ben said. 'Let's get this show started.'

Rowan got as far as laying her suitcase out on her bed and then realising that almost all of the clothes she'd been wearing were either Willow's or bought with Willow's credit card, and stopped. Instead of packing, she stretched out on the side of the bed not currently covered by a suitcase, and reached for her phone.

'Rowan? What's going on?' Willow asked. 'I've got, like, eight voicemails on my phone from Ben, suddenly telling me he knows everything, and then you weren't answering yours and—'

'He doesn't know about the baby,' Rowan said quickly. 'He does know I'm not you.'

'How?'

Rowan explained the events of the morning. Willow did not seem to be focusing on the most important parts.

'Wait, so Eli was naked in bed with you when Ben walked in? Oh, my God! When did this happen? What's the deal with the two of you? Is this a drunken hook-up or something more…?'

'It's…not a drunken hook-up.' Rowan felt her cheeks heat up and hoped that the video on her phone didn't show the blush. From the wide smile that split Willow's face, she suspected it did.

'So it's something more.' On the video, Willow sat up straighter at Rowan's kitchen table, in Rowan's little cottage, in Rowan's village of Rumbelow, and said, 'Tell me everything.'

Rowan opened her mouth to do just that. But what came out was, 'What's the point? I'm packing to come home right now. So, whatever it was, I just have to leave it here in New York.'

Willow's eyes widened on the screen. 'Okay. This is clearly a conversation that needs tea. Go put the kettle on, and I'll do the same, and while it's brewing you can tell me exactly what's been going on over there between the two of you.'

She reached for the teapot from the top shelf in such an easy, familiar movement that Rowan almost cried. That was her teapot. Her cottage. She should be there doing this for Willow, the way it had always been. Willow had the adventures, and Rowan heard about them later over pots of tea.

Now, everything was different.

'I don't know where to begin,' she admitted.

'Start from the beginning,' Willow advised. 'Right from the moment you arrived in New York and found him in my apartment. Because I'm pretty sure you've been leaving things out in your accounts of your Big Apple adventures, haven't you?'

Rowan couldn't deny it. So, instead, she told her sister everything—from the first panic attack to the realisation that their time was almost over, and their race home to bed, and onto their rude awakening that morning.

Willow mostly listened—although, being Willow, she obviously had to interject with a few important observations. Like, 'I knew this wasn't just all about some dress you made!' And, 'Wait, there's a unicorn in New York?'

'Well, it all sounds pretty much fairy-tale-perfect to me,' Willow said when she'd finished. 'Up until the part where my ex-boy-friend walked in. But he's *my* problem, not yours. So why aren't you happy? Why aren't you loved-up and making dresses for celeb-rities and living your best life with Eli right now?'

'Because…' When she put it like that, what she needed to do sounded obvious. But Rowan knew it wasn't. Maybe it could have been for Willow, but she *wasn't* Willow.

And that was the point.

She took a deep breath and tried to explain. 'When I came here, I was pretending to be you. So I lived life as if I *was* you, as best as I could. I took chances and put myself out there…all that stuff I haven't done since I walked out on you and Mum years ago. And I know… I know that was probably the idea— and don't think we're not going to have a conversation about why you decided sending me to New York was the best solution to your situation because we are, once I'm over this particular crisis.'

'I have no idea what you're talking about,' Willow said, far too innocently. 'But go on.'

'These last weeks here in New York… they haven't felt like real life. My real life is *there,* in Rumbelow. And the person I've been here… I can't be sure if she's real either. I miss my cottage, my home. And I miss the person I am there too, a little.'

'So come home,' Willow said. 'Leave Eli behind as a fond memory. A holiday fling.'

'I would. Except…'

'Except you're in love with him,' Willow crowed triumphantly, almost upsetting her cup of tea as she thumped the table with one hand.

Love?

Oh, God, Rowan hadn't even really *thought* about love. Love definitely felt like one of those things that was for other people. She hadn't been looking for it, even here, on her escape from reality.

She'd fallen for Eli in increments. One touch, one word, one insight at a time. Until she was in so deep it was hard to see a way out.

'Oh, God, I'm in love with Eli.'

But did it change anything?

No. Not really.

'I still can't stay here.'

'Why not?' Willow demanded. 'You love him, you're glowing, he makes you happy, it's the greatest city in the world, you've conquered your fear of being out there again... You *can* do this, Ro.'

And she was right, Rowan realised. She could. But *should* she?

'I... I feel like two people right now, Will. The old Rumbelow Rowan, and the new New York one,' she said, trying to explain. 'I need to find a way to make those two people one, before I can really move forward with my life.'

'And you need to come back to Rumbelow to do that?'

'I think so. Yes.'

Maybe not for ever. But she needed to get her head straight before she made any huge, life-changing decisions for herself—or for Eli.

She wasn't a city person. She didn't *want* to be either. But she couldn't imagine Eli anywhere except New York.

And if there was something going on with the family business…this was where he was going to need to be. She'd already caused enough friction between him and his brother—not to mention Ben and Willow. The person she'd been here in New York might have wanted to be altruistic and compassionate—giving to Launch, helping out at the Castaway Café, making Kelly's dress—but in the end she'd been selfish.

She'd given in to what she wanted—Eli—rather than holding out and doing what was right, even knowing how much it could cost Willow, and even Eli himself.

And she wasn't sure *that* was the version of Rowan she wanted to be.

'Then come home.' Willow's smile on the phone screen was gentle. 'You have to be sure, and you have to feel right about the decisions you're making. That's why *I* came here, after all. So come home and see if Rumbelow can work its magic on you.'

'Did it do that for you?' Rowan asked.

Willow nodded. 'Yeah, I think it did. I'm ready to face the music now, anyway. This place has taught me what I want, and now all that's left is to make it happen.'

'That's good.' Rowan wanted to ask exactly *what* Rumbelow had taught her twin, but the closed look on her face stopped her. Willow would tell her, when she was ready.

'Perhaps Eli will come to Rumbelow with you,' Willow said hopefully.

'Perhaps,' Rowan echoed.

But she knew as she said it, it wasn't true.

This was something she needed to do on her own.

Eli returned to the apartment to find Rowan's bags already packed by the door.

'You're leaving?' he asked, as she appeared from the bedroom with the last of her things.

She answered with another question. 'What happened at the board meeting?'

Heavy with the memory of one of the least enjoyable afternoons of his life, Eli sank down to sit on the sofa. Rowan settled beside him, and just her hand on his arm made him feel a little better.

'The board had evidence that Ben had been making some...not illegal, but not entirely sensible or ethical decisions, behind their backs. Keeping things from them as far as the terms would allow. They were…unhappy.' To put things very, very mildly.

He'd never seen his godfather so angry. And he'd been one of the more reasonable board members in attendance.

'What did they do?' Rowan asked. 'I mean, I don't really understand how boards of companies operate, but I guess they had the power to do something about it?'

Eli nodded. He wasn't sure *he* really understood how big corporations—or at least O'Donnell Industries—operated either. It wasn't as if his father had ever taught him, the way he'd taught Ben, and his experience and education was mostly in the non-profit sector. According to Jeremiah, the way their father had left the business—the uneven split between the brothers, the power that remained with the board—wasn't exactly typical anyway. So no, he didn't really understand how it worked.

But it looked as if he was going to have to learn.

He'd taken his eye off the ball. He'd avoided his brother for weeks because of his guilt over his feelings for Rowan—especially when he'd thought she was still Willow. And maybe this had been going on for longer, but the point was, he hadn't been paying attention. Hadn't noticed the hole his brother was digging for himself and the company, because he'd been too caught up in his attraction to Rowan.

He'd gone after a woman he knew he shouldn't want. And even when he'd learnt her true identity, he'd kept lying to everyone all the same, even though he knew it was the wrong thing to do. All because he hadn't been ready to say goodbye to her.

This mess was at least partly his fault. And it was his responsibility to put it right.

'They wanted him to step down—resign in disgrace—I think. But we managed to reach a compromise.' He took a deep breath. 'They want me to run the company with him. Keep him on the straight and narrow, and get the company's reputation back where it belongs.'

It had turned out that Ben's cut corners and underhand dealings were getting them quite a name for themselves on the internet, and before long it would be in the papers too. That was what the board wanted to avoid most of all.

Rowan winced, and patted his thigh sympathetically. 'Working with your brother. That's going to be... What about Launch?'

He sighed. 'I've got a great team in place

there. I'll still be involved, but I'm going to have to scale back the time I can spend there, until I can get O'Donnell Industries back on track.'

It was going to be a steep learning curve too. Eli relished a challenge, normally. But right now... Right now, he just wanted to pack his own case and go wherever Rowan was heading, and say to hell with the company.

Was that so bad of him?

He knew he wouldn't do it, though.

Whatever his father might have thought of him, he was still the only father he'd ever known. This company was the legacy he'd left him, even if only a sliver of it.

And the company wasn't just his father's either. As Jeremiah had reminded him, it was his mother's passion too, for a long time, when they were young and just married and building it up together. Eli had a right to it.

None of that was why he was doing it, though.

He was doing it for Ben, even if his brother didn't appreciate that right now.

To be the brother he *should* have been all along. And maybe to model to Ben that there were other ways to be the head of a company, other than the way their father had. Other ways to live. Other ways to be a person, even.

'How did Ben take it?' Rowan asked, as if reading his mind.

That called for another sigh. Because this was the really difficult part.

'Badly. He…he doesn't have much of a say in the matter, because the board have the power to appoint me to the role regardless.'

Rowan frowned. 'He could make things difficult, though?'

'He could,' Eli said. 'But I'm hoping he'll see reason. Eventually. But there's another problem to deal with first.'

Rowan stared at him for a moment, then her eyes widened. 'He's gone to find Willow?'

'I'm afraid so.' Eli wasn't entirely sure how the two situations had got conflated in Ben's head, but they had. 'He seems to think that this is all our fault—the three of us, I mean. That if Willow had just been there to hang off his arm and smooth situations over and convince people that he was a settled, responsible man—or at least that his celebrity mattered more than what he was doing with the company—it would all have worked out for him.'

'I'm guessing that people seeing us together and thinking I was Willow didn't help the situation either?'

'Not exactly. Basically, he thinks we all set out to trash his reputation, and now he's off to yell at Willow about it to make himself feel better.' He *hoped* yelling was the worst of it. He didn't believe his brother would hurt another person, let alone a pregnant woman, but he didn't like the idea of Willow waiting there for him alone either.

'Does he know where she is?' Rowan asked.

'Not yet. But I can't imagine it'll take him long to find out.' Ben still had all the connections of the company, and his own personal ones. Now he knew to look, he could probably have Willow's location in a matter of hours.

Rowan got to her feet. 'Then it's just as well I've got a flight home late tonight. I just need to call a taxi to the airport.'

'I'll take you,' Eli said, even though the last thing he wanted was to send her away.

If he could keep her here, with him, for ever, he would, he realised. He'd get down on one knee right now if it would make her stay.

And maybe it would. But it wouldn't be the right thing to do.

She needed to go.

They'd made this mess. Maybe not alone. And perhaps it wasn't their fault they'd been drawn into it all the same.

But they'd made the whole situation worse by falling for each other. Choosing each other now would be selfish, and it could have even more catastrophic results for Ben and Willow and their futures.

Right now, they had to keep their focus where it belonged—on helping their siblings, who needed them more than ever. They had to take the responsibility for muddying the waters and causing more pain and hurt.

And they had to fix it.

Their fingers met on the handle of her suitcase, and when Rowan looked up at him he saw tears in her eyes.

'I don't want to go,' she admitted.

'I want you to stay. But I know you need to go.' They'd talked a lot the night before, in between everything else. He knew how torn she felt, between the woman she'd been in Rumbelow and the woman she was here. How she didn't want to be Willow, but she wasn't sure how to be Rowan any more either.

That was something she needed to figure

out for herself. And he had to give her the space to do it.

'I want you to come with me,' Rowan said with a very small smile. 'But I know you need to stay.'

'I do.' And he cursed his brother for that. But also… New York was his home. Could he really give that up—turn his back on everything he'd built there, all the work there was still to do—and move to England, just to be with her? What would he even do in a fishing village?

No, there was too much work here in New York for him to walk away.

'So…' Rowan trailed off. He didn't blame her.

'We'll go and do the things we need to do,' he said.

'Apart.'

'Yeah.'

'Well, that sucks.' She sighed again. 'I can't help but feel that me coming here, pretending to be Willow…it's actually made things worse, not better. For her, but for everyone else too.'

He knew what she meant. Willow had wanted time to decide on her future so she could discuss it rationally with Ben with a clear head, and instead she'd get him flying in furious and spoiling for any fight he could win. Not to mention that Rowan being her had given them both a taste of something they couldn't have—and that would leave them both wanting.

And yet…

They were saying goodbye. He might never see her again. So he wasn't going to let her leave on a lie.

He gripped her hand tight. 'I wouldn't change it, though. Not for the world. Not if it meant never getting to know you.'

She met his gaze, and this time her eyes weren't the only ones that were wet with tears. 'Neither would I.'

CHAPTER THIRTEEN

RUMBELOW WAS GLORIOUS in the sunshine. The waves in the harbour glittered in the sunlight, the brightly coloured boats bobbing gently on the sea. The cobblestone streets were lined with bistro tables and tourists eating breakfast, bunting and flags strung well above head height, zigzagging across the paths. The air was filled with the scents of freshly baked bread, coffee and the ever-present tang of salt.

Rowan waved to one of the shopkeepers as she passed, and smiled as they called out a good morning. It *was* a good morning. It was an almost perfect morning in the village she loved. Her home.

It just didn't seem to have quite the same magic as she remembered from before she went away.

Willow had returned to New York not long after Rowan came back here—although not before Ben had tracked her down. Still, her twin seemed to have that whole situation under control—she was more steady and settled than Rowan had thought her capable of being. It had gone a long way to assuaging her guilt about making Willow's situation worse—as had a lengthy heart-to-heart with her after Ben had left again, where her twin had reminded her that it wasn't all or nothing. She could be a loving sister *and* have whatever life she wanted. Willow had never wanted her to mortgage her own happiness for her.

Besides, looking out at the old lifeboat station now as she turned the corner towards her cottage, Rowan suspected Willow would be back in Rumbelow sooner rather than later.

Probably not to stay, though. Hardly anybody did.

Rumbelow was a place for locals and for tourists. The tourists came in their droves in the summer months, then disappeared with the sunshine. While they were there, the streets buzzed with activity, with noise—and with money. There were never enough hands to do everything, and always more people than space. But when they were gone... Rumbelow was a different place altogether.

The locals stayed year-round, despite the

weather or the storms, or the empty holiday homes standing forlornly on the edge of the sea. They stayed when the fish weren't biting, or when the sea raged and breached the walls. In many cases, they'd stayed for generations already, and would stay for generations more.

Or they wouldn't.

People left, of course they did. For love or work or opportunities—or just to see the wider world. Nobody blamed them for that, and they were always welcome to come home and visit.

And then there were people like her. Transplants. People who came as tourists and stayed. They never quite became local, but they were the nearest thing.

When she'd settled down in Rumbelow, she'd never imagined leaving. It was her safe place, her haven. Her cottage was her sanctuary. She loved the winter months best of all, because the village emptied out and she could batten down her hatches against the weather and stay hidden away.

She'd thought that would be enough for her for ever.

But now…

Willow and her schemes had given her a taste of the outside world again. And while she knew she never wanted to go back to the kind of high profile, visible career she'd had before, knowing that she *could* do it without breaking was a surprisingly potent thing.

The world was bigger than Rumbelow. And she wasn't too small and scared to enjoy it any more.

You're just making excuses because you miss Eli.

The voice in her head could be her own or it could be Willow's but, either way, she couldn't deny the pull in her heart that led her back to New York. But could she really live in a city again? Give up all of this? This life she'd worked so hard to build for herself?

She sighed as she turned into her garden gate, ready to trudge up the path to her cottage door...

And stopped.

Because there, on her doorstep, sat a tired-looking Eli, licking an ice cream cone from Marco's.

'You might be right,' he said, as he got to his feet. 'I didn't think it was possible, but this *is* better than Giovanni's.'

She took a cautious step forward, half afraid that he was some sort of mirage that would disappear if she got close enough to touch.

'What are you doing here?' she asked.

'I shouldn't be,' he admitted. 'I should be back in New York. There's a million things still to straighten out with the company, and Ben is being...well, Ben, and the board as a whole are generally making things difficult, which my godfather seems to find endlessly amusing, so I really should be in New York. But...'

Rowan's heart seemed to swell in her chest. 'But?'

'I missed you,' he said simply. 'And I know you belong here, so I came to you.'

Rowan stared at him so long that Eli started to worry he'd said something wrong.

'The thing is... I'm not sure that I do any more. Belong here, I mean.'

He blinked. 'You're not?'

He hadn't come here with any expectations. Hadn't even allowed himself much in the way of hope. He'd just needed to see her, that was all.

Running the company with Ben was...it felt like jumping from a skyscraper and hoping someone would be there to catch him. It was hard and intense and even though he *knew* it was the right thing to do, he also knew it could take over his life if he let it.

Could turn him into the sort of man his father had been and his brother had been becoming, before he'd stepped in.

Eli couldn't risk that. He needed to hold onto the important things. The things that mattered.

The *people* that mattered.

When he was with Rowan he felt grounded. He felt at ease. At home.

He'd thought home was New York. Now, he was starting to believe it was wherever she was. And Rumbelow looked like a nice enough place. With a good Wi-Fi connection and regular red-eye flights back to the States, he could probably make it work. The ice cream alone was pretty good compensation.

Except now she was saying she didn't belong here. What was he supposed to make of that?

'I thought that Rumbelow was where I needed to be, because it was where I was safe. Where I felt protected and secure. But I realised, coming back here, that what it really gave me was a place to hide,' Rowan explained. 'And I don't want to hide any more.

Not from who I am, or what I can do—or from who I love.'

Her voice grew stronger with every word and Eli found himself drawn nearer, without meaning to, until his arms were around her waist and her gaze was locked on his.

He saw everything he'd ever hoped for in her eyes. But he still needed to hear the words.

'What does that mean for us? Am I going to be eating Giovanni's or Marco's ice cream this summer?'

She smiled, a dimple appearing in her cheek. 'How about both?'

He raised his eyebrows. 'Both?'

'Yes. Both.' She took a quick breath, before the words came tumbling out. 'I've already wound up my dress commissions here. And I even answered some of those emails and voicemails. I've got meetings set up in New York next week.'

His heart stuttered in his chest. 'You were coming back anyway?'

She gave him a shy nod. 'Yeah. Is that okay?'

'It's better than okay,' he said fervently. 'It's everything.'

'I want to be close to Willow and the baby, wherever they end up. And I want to be out in the world again, not just in this tiny bubble of safety I've built myself. I'll always want to come back here too—it's a place that means so much to me. But most of all… I want to be with you. Wherever that is.'

'That's the conclusion that got me on that plane last night, straight out of my last meeting, without even an overnight bag,' Eli admitted. 'I had to buy a toothbrush at the airport. I just had to see you.'

'I don't ever want to go two weeks without seeing you again,' Rowan said—and then she was in his arms and kissing him and Eli knew that it didn't matter *where* they were, as long as they were together.

'Then we won't,' he promised, when they finally pulled apart. 'We can split our time between here and New York—and anywhere else in the world you want to be. Of course…' He grinned as the thought occurred to him, the weight of the box in his pocket a happy reminder. 'All that international travel…the passport controls would be easier if we had the same surname.'

She raised her eyebrows at him. 'Is that seriously the most romantic proposal you could manage?'

'How about this?' He dropped to one knee and, fishing the ring box from his pocket, opened it to reveal the ring he'd travelled thousands of miles to give her.

Rowan's hands flew to her mouth as her eyes widened. 'Yes!'

Okay, he could have phrased that better.

'Yes, it's more romantic, or yes—?'

'Yes to all of it.' Rowan bent down to kiss him again. 'I'm only saying yes to things from now on. And a life with you is something I could never say no to.'

* * * * *

Look out for the next story in
the Twin Sister Swap duet
Socialite's Nine-Month Secret

And if you enjoyed this story,
check out these other great reads
from Sophie Pembroke

Best Man with Benefits
Baby Surprise in Costa Rica
Their Icelandic Marriage Reunion

All available now!